Scene of the Crime

ENGLISH TRANSLATIONS OF WORKS
BY PATRICK MODIANO

From Yale University Press
After the Circus
Family Record
Invisible Ink
Little Jewel
Paris Nocturne
Pedigree: A Memoir
Scene of the Crime
Sleep of Memory
Such Fine Boys
Sundays in August
Suspended Sentences: Three Novellas (Afterimage, Suspended
    Sentences, and Flowers of Ruin)

Also Available
The Black Notebook
Catherine Certitude
Dora Bruder
Honeymoon
In the Café of Lost Youth
Lacombe Lucien
Missing Person
The Occupation Trilogy (The Night Watch, Ring Roads, and La
    Place de l'Etoile)
Out of the Dark
So You Don't Get Lost in the Neighborhood
28 Paradises (with Dominique Zehrfuss)
Villa Triste
Young Once

PATRICK MODIANO

Scene of the Crime

A NOVEL

Translated from the French by
Mark Polizzotti

A MARGELLOS
WORLD REPUBLIC OF LETTERS BOOK

Yale UNIVERSITY PRESS | NEW HAVEN & LONDON

English translation copyright © 2023 by Mark Polizzotti.

Originally published as *Chevreuse*. © Editions GALLIMARD, Paris, 2021.

Yale University Press books may be purchased in quantity for
educational, business, or promotional use. For information, please
e-mail sales.press@yale.edu (US office) or sales@yaleup.co.uk
(UK office).

Set in Source Serif type by Karen Stickler.
Printed in Great Britain by T Books Ltd, Padstow, Cornwall.

Library of Congress Control Number: 2022937804
ISBN 978-0-300-26593-4 (hardcover : alk. paper)

A catalogue record for this book is available from the
British Library.

10 9 8 7 6 5 4 3 2 1

For Dominique

How many names have I etched in memory
like "dog" or "elephant" or "cow"
So long ago now, I recognize them only from afar,
even the zebra—and what was it all for?

RAINER MARIA RILKE

Scene of the Crime

Bosmans recalled that a single word, "Chevreuse," kept cropping up in the conversation. And that a song played constantly on the radio that autumn, sung by a certain Serge Latour. He'd heard it in the small, empty Vietnamese restaurant, one evening when he was with the woman he called Deathmask.

Gentle lady
So often do I dream of you . . .

That evening, "Deathmask" had closed her eyes, visibly moved by the song's lyrics and the singer's voice. The restaurant, its radio on the counter playing nonstop, was located in one of the narrow streets between Maubert-Mutualité and the Seine.

Other lyrics, other faces, and even verses he'd read at the time jostled together in his head—verses so numerous he couldn't write them all down:

"The lock of chestnut hair . . . " " . . . From Boulevard de la Chapelle, from fair Montmartre and Auteuil . . . "

Auteuil. That was a name that rang strangely for him. Auteuil. But how could he marshal all those signals and Morse code messages that stretched over a distance of more than fifty years? What was the common thread?

He jotted down thoughts as they flitted through his mind. Generally in the morning or late afternoon. It took only a detail, one that might have seemed insignificant to anyone else. That was it: a detail. The word "thought" wasn't right. Too solemn. A multitude of details gradually filled entire pages of his blue notebook, apparently having no connection with one another, and so cursory that they would have been incomprehensible to someone trying to read them.

The more these seemingly unrelated details accumulated on the blank pages, the greater his chances of elucidating them later on—he was sure of it. And their apparently futile character must not discourage him.

His teacher had once told him, back in the day, that the different stages of life—childhood, youth, middle age, senescence—corresponded to several successive deaths. It was the same for the scraps of memory he tried to set down as fast as he could: scattered images from a period of his life that he watched flit by before they disappeared forever into oblivion.

Chevreuse. Perhaps that name would draw other names to him, like a magnet. Bosmans repeated it in a whisper: "Chevreuse." And what if he held the thread that would let him reel in the entire spool? But why Chevreuse? There had been a Duchess de Chevreuse, of course, who figured in Cardinal de Retz's *Memoirs*, long one of his favorite bedside readings. One January Sunday in those distant years, stepping off a crowded train returning from Normandy, he had left the white-covered volume printed on Bible paper on his seat in the compartment, and he'd known immediately he would never get over that loss. The next morning, he had gone to the Gare Saint-Lazare and wandered around the waiting room, the shops, finally coming upon the lost-and-found window. The man behind the counter had handed him the volume of Cardinal de Retz's *Memoirs*, intact, the red ribbon marker clearly visible where he had interrupted his reading the day before on the train.

He had left the station, shoving the book deep in a pocket of his coat for fear of losing it again. A sunny Jan-

uary morning. The earth continued to turn and the passersby to walk all around him at their tranquil pace—at
least in his memory. After Trinité Church, he arrived at
the bottom of what he called "the first slopes." Now he
only needed follow his usual path, climbing toward Pigalle and Montmartre.

In a Montmartre street in those years, he had crossed
paths one afternoon with Serge Latour, the man who
sang "Gentle Lady." That encounter—barely a few seconds—had been such a minuscule detail in Bosmans's
life that he was amazed it resurfaced in his memory.

Why Serge Latour? He hadn't spoken to him, and
anyway, what would he have said? That a girlfriend of
his, "Deathmask," used to hum "Gentle Lady"? Or ask
whether the song's title had been inspired by a medie-
val poet and musician named Guillaume de Machaut?
Three 45s on Polydor in one year. He didn't know what
had since become of Serge Latour. Soon after that fleeting encounter, he'd heard someone in Montmartre say
that Serge Latour "was touring around Morocco, Spain,
and Ibiza," as was common back then. And the remark,
in the hubbub of conversations, had remained suspended for all eternity; he could still hear it fifty years
later, as clearly as on that evening, uttered by a voice
that would forever remain anonymous. Yes, whatever
had become of Serge Latour? And that strange girlfriend
nicknamed Deathmask? Thinking of those two individu-

als was enough to make him even more sensitive to the dust—or rather, the odor—of time.

Leaving Chevreuse, there's a bend in the road, then a narrow tree-lined highway. After a few miles, the entrance to a village, and soon you were running alongside train tracks. But very few trains passed over them. One at around 5 a.m., which they called the "rose train," since it carried that variety of flower from the regional nurseries to Paris; the other train at 9:15 p.m. sharp. The small station looked abandoned. To the right, opposite the station, an alley rising in a slope past an empty lot led to Rue du Docteur-Kurzenne. In that street, slightly to the left, was the front of a house.

On the old Geological Survey map, the distances did not match Bosmans's recollection. Chevreuse in his memories wasn't as far from Rue du Docteur-Kurzenne as it was on the map. Behind the house on Rue du Docteur-Kurzenne were three terraced gardens. A rusty iron gate in the wall surrounding the highest one opened onto a clearing, then came the grounds that were said to belong to the Mauvières chateau, a few miles away.

Bosmans had often walked far down the forest paths, without ever reaching the chateau.

If the Geological Survey map contradicted his memory of the place, it was no doubt because he had passed through the area in various stages of his life, and the years had ended up shortening the distances. Moreover, it was said that the game warden of the Mauvières chateau had once lived in the house on Rue du Docteur-Kurzenne, which was why that house had always seemed like a border post to him, with Rue du Docteur-Kurzenne marking the boundaries of a domain—or rather, a principality of forests, ponds, woods, and parks—named Chevreuse. He tried to reconstruct a kind of Geological Survey map of his own, but with holes, blanks, villages, and back roads that no longer existed. Little by little, the routes came back to him. One in particular seemed quite precise. A car trip, its point of departure an apartment somewhere near Porte d'Auteuil. People gathered there in late afternoon, often after dark. The ones who seemed to live there permanently were a man of about forty, a small boy who must have been his son, and a young woman who worked as the boy's nanny. She and the boy occupied the room at the back of the apartment.

Some fifteen years later, Bosmans thought he recognized that man, alone and grown older, through the window of a Wimpy's on the Champs-Elysées. He had gone inside and sat next to him, as often happened in self-service restaurants. He wanted to ask for explanations, but he suddenly experienced a memory gap: he couldn't recall the man's name. Besides, bringing up the apartment in Auteuil and the people Bosmans had once met there might have embarrassed him. And what had become of the boy? And the girl, whose name was Kim? That evening, in Wimpy's, a detail had caught his attention: the man was wearing a huge wristwatch with multiple dials that Bosmans couldn't stop staring at. The other noticed and pressed a button at the bottom of the watch, which triggered a soft chime, no doubt an alarm. He smiled, and his smile, that watch, and that chime evoked a childhood memory.

It was Deathmask who had brought him to the apartment in Auteuil one evening. She had acquired the nickname, long before they met, owing to her impassive nature, and because she often remained silent and inscrutable.

In her soft voice, she would sometimes say by way of introduction, "You can call me Deathmask." Her real name was Camille. And whenever he thought of her, Bosmans hesitated between writing Camille or Deathmask. He preferred Camille.

At first, he couldn't quite fathom what all those people in the Auteuil apartment had in common. Did they meet via the "network," a disused telephone number over which disembodied voices made assignations under false names? Camille, aka Deathmask, had told him of this "network" and of the disused telephone number AUTEUIL 15-28, which by a strange coincidence, she said, used to be the apartment's phone number. And that apartment, despite the fugitive presence of the child and the young girl in the back room, apparently was not really lived in, but rather served as a meeting place and a site for brief encounters.

Among the people gathered in the living room, a room furnished with three large, low-slung sofas, with a double door that opened curiously onto a bathroom— among those people who were no more than shadows in his memory, because of the light in the apartment that was always too dim, Camille aka Deathmask had introduced him to a friend of hers, a certain Martine Hayward, whom she seemed to have known for a long time.

A late afternoon in summer, when daylight would last until ten o'clock. The three of them had left the apartment. A car was parked a little farther up the street, Martine Hayward's car. Deathmask had sat behind the wheel. The nickname didn't really suit her, but she retained it out of a perverse sense of humor.

"Would you mind if we swing by the Vallée de Chevreuse?" Martine Hayward had asked her, sitting next to him in the back seat. "Just a pit stop."

For much of the trip, Camille had kept silent.

"We are now entering the Vallée de Chevreuse," Camille had said that late afternoon, turning toward him. The landscape had changed, as if they had crossed a frontier. And from then on, whenever he followed that same route from Paris and Porte d'Auteuil, he would experience the same feeling: the sense of gliding into a fresh zone that the foliage on the trees sheltered from the sun. And in winter, because of the snow which was heavier in the Vallée de Chevreuse than anywhere else, it was as if you were driving along mountain roads.

A few miles before Chevreuse proper, Camille aka Deathmask turned onto a path in the woods, the entrance to which was marked by a wooden sign bearing the half-faded inscription: "Moulin-de-Vert-Cœur Inn." An arrow pointed the way.

She had parked the car in front of a large half-timbered structure. On its flank, a restaurant dining room with picture windows. Martine Hayward got out of the car.

"I'll just be a minute."

He and Camille remained seated for a while. And when Martine Hayward still hadn't returned, they got out of the car as well.

Camille told him that Martine Hayward's husband owned this Moulin-de-Vert-Cœur Inn, but the establishment had gone bust—too many administrative complications and upkeep costs, debts, not enough guests, and anyway, Martine Hayward's husband wasn't much of a hotel keeper or restaurateur. They'd had to close the hotel, then the restaurant. Now it was just a dilapidated building, looking like a Norman villa washed up in the Vallée de Chevreuse. A pane was missing from one of the picture windows.

Bosmans had questioned Camille about this Hayward person, but she answered evasively. He was abroad for the moment, but would be back in France soon. While he was away, Martine Hayward found it hard to live alone in that huge abandoned inn. Camille had offered to move into one of the fifteen empty guest rooms and live with her, at least until her husband returned, but meanwhile Martine Hayward had found a small house to rent in the vicinity.

She reappeared, holding a black leather suitcase, which she put down on the stoop to turn the key in the heavy wooden front door, as if she were the final guest, responsible for shutting down the Moulin-de-Vert-Cœur Inn forever.

Camille took her place behind the wheel. And Martine Hayward in the back seat, next to him.

"Now I'll show you the way," she had said.

They had to rejoin the road and follow it east to Toussus-le-Noble. It suddenly occurred to Bosmans that he knew that name, but he couldn't say why. When they skirted the airfield, it all became clear. The name "Toussus-le-Noble" called to mind an airshow he'd seen, one Sunday in his childhood. Unless that was at Villacoublay, the other aerodrome nearby. He didn't have the exact map of the region in his head, but for him those two airfields marked the limits of the Vallée de Chevreuse. Besides, after Toussus-le-Noble, the light changed, and you entered another region of which the Vallée de Chevreuse was the backcountry.

"One more quick detour and we'll head back to Paris," Martine Hayward said to him, as if in apology.

They arrived in Buc. Bosmans felt a stab in his heart. This name, which he had forgotten, that brief, clear name, seemed to waken him brutally from a long sleep. He wanted to confide to them that he had lived near here, but it was none of their business.

At the entrance to the next village, Bosmans immediately recognized the town hall and the railroad crossing. Deathmask drove over the crossing and took the main street to the church square. She stopped in front of the church where he had been a choirboy one Christmas night. Martine Hayward said it would be better to turn around and follow the railroad tracks. They couldn't miss coming to the train station and the road facing it, as she'd been instructed.

The public garden ran alongside the tracks. The concrete barriers and thickets separating it from the road hadn't changed. Bosmans had traveled fifteen years into the past, as if a period of his childhood was about to begin again. And yet the public garden was much smaller than the one in his memory, where they sent him to play during summer vacations, at nightfall. The station also struck him as tiny, and its decrepit façade brought home how much time had passed.

Camille turned the car onto the rising alley. Then he felt his heart pound. To the left, the empty lot still deserved the nickname "the forest primeval," as in the days when he and his playmates from the Jeanne d'Arc school would venture in until they nearly got lost. The vegetation was even denser.

She parked at the corner of Rue du Docteur-Kurzenne. A woman in a black blouse was waiting at the iron gate and fence of number 38. Martine Hayward waved and walked toward her. The woman had a folder under her arm. Camille also got out of the car, while he remained in the back seat. But when he saw the woman take a key-ring from her bag and open the iron gate, he decided to join them. This way, he'd get to the bottom of it. He repeated the expression to himself, "the bottom of it," to fully understand what it meant, and perhaps to buck up his courage.

Martine Hayward introduced him to the woman in the black blouse: "A friend of mine, Jean Bosmans," and Camille turned to him with a smile: "This is the woman from the real estate agency." But standing in front of this house after so many years made him feel slightly dizzy.

He followed them to the front porch. The woman in the black blouse unlocked the front door that hadn't changed in fifteen years. Still with its pale blue color and, at the center, the gilded metal of the mail slot. She stood aside to let Camille and Martine Hayward enter. And him too. He hesitated a few seconds before saying he'd wait for them outside.

He found himself alone, across the street, facing the house. Nearly seven o'clock. The sun was still fairly strong, as at the end of those summer days when he'd played in the wide expanse of tall grass around the ruined chateau, then followed the road to return home. Those late afternoons, the silence around him was so deep that he could hear the regular clack of his sandals on the sidewalk.

He had returned under the same sun and in the same silence. He would have liked to join the three others in the house, but he couldn't summon the courage. Or walk a few steps down the sloping path to see whether the weeping willow still occupied the same spot behind the large gate on the left. But he preferred to wait there, motionless, rather than walk aimlessly in an abandoned village. And then he ended up convincing himself that he was dreaming, the way you dream about certain places where you once lived. And that dream, fortunately, he could interrupt whenever he wished.

The three women came out of the house, the one in the black blouse in the lead. And he felt a sudden disquiet: he was witnessing the end of a police raid and they didn't know he'd lived there. Otherwise, they would have demanded an explanation. But Camille waved and smiled at him. It was only a humdrum visit to a rental property that in any case was no longer the same. They must have changed the arrangement of the rooms, knocked down partitions, painted the walls a different color. And in that house, not a trace of him remained.

The woman in the black blouse walked them to the car parked on the corner. She handed her folder and a set of keys to Martine Hayward, specifying which key opened which door. New keys, smaller than the ones from before. So they didn't open the same doors. The old keys were gone. Deathmask, Martine Hayward, and the woman in the black blouse would never have a clue.

On the way back, Camille was again at the wheel. She talked about the house and its various rooms. Martine Hayward wondered whether she shouldn't move into the ground floor, as that "bedroom" was bigger than the others. And yet Bosmans didn't recall there being any bedroom on the ground floor. The front door opened onto a hallway. At the end of it, the stairway. To the right, the living room and its bow window. To the left, the dining room. They also mentioned the three terraced gardens in back of the house. So they were still there. And the grave of Doctor Guillotin in the first garden? He suddenly felt like asking questions, but he forced himself not to say a word. How would they react if they learned that he'd lived in that house? Why would they care? All this was extremely banal. Except for him.

It wasn't the same route they'd come down by. They didn't cross through the Vallée de Chevreuse, but instead skirted the Villacoublay airfield via a local road. And this route had been so familiar to him fifteen years earlier—this route he'd taken by car, by bus, and later on foot when he ran away from boarding school—that he felt as if everything was starting over, without his being able to define exactly what. There would never be anything new in his life. But that fear, which he felt for the first time, had already dissipated by the time they reached Petit-Clamart.

"You should have come in with us to see the house," Martine Hayward said to him. "Don't you agree, Camille?"

"Yeah, I didn't get why you stayed outside by yourself."

Despite all the years, he could still hear Camille's gentle, drawling voice saying that sentence that he still remembered precisely: "I didn't get why you stayed outside by yourself." Her words probably hadn't struck him at the time, but their echo resounded in his memory and corresponded to an attitude, or rather a way of being, that he'd had since childhood and long afterward, and maybe still had today.

He hadn't known what to answer Martine Hayward or Camille, and Martine Hayward had given him a peculiar look, or so he'd thought at the time. She had placed the folder the woman in the black blouse had given her between them on the seat. In Boulogne, Camille braked suddenly so as not to run a red light. The folder slid off the seat and the sheets scattered. He picked them up one by one and, as they were numbered, put them back in order. He saw it was a rental contract and inventory for the house. The letterhead on the first page gave the names of the agency and its manager, who must have been the woman in the black blouse. But another name jumped out at him, that of the homeowner: ROSE-MARIE KRAWELL. So she was still alive and the house was still hers. That knowledge made him feel so agitated that he felt like telling them about it. But what exactly could he say? And how could it possibly interest them?

He handed the red folder to Martine Hayward after replacing the sheets. She thanked him, still giving him that peculiar look.

"Do you know the owner?" he blurted.

And he immediately regretted having said it, like someone kicking himself for losing his cool.

"The owner? No, why?"

Martine Hayward had answered in a curt tone. Apparently his question bothered her.

"I think René-Marco knows her," said Deathmask. "I seem to recall she's a friend of his."

"You must be right. In any case, it was René-Marco who pointed me to the real estate agency."

And then there was a long silence among the three of them, which he wanted to break but he couldn't find the words. They had stopped at Porte Molitor, at the border of Boulogne and Auteuil, and he remembered he'd been born around there. The week before, he'd gone to the town hall in Boulogne-Billancourt because he needed a copy of his birth certificate. No question about it, in the last few days the past was making itself felt, a past he'd long forgotten. In Auteuil, Camille parked just in front of the building in which the apartment occupied the third or fourth floor. It was about 9 p.m., but it was still light.

"Are you sleeping over at René-Marco's?"

"Yes," Martine Hayward had answered.

So did the apartment belong to the aforementioned René-Marco? Surely this was the man of about forty, whom he'd later learn was the father of the little boy, the child who occupied the back room.

"In that case, I'll stay here tonight too," Camille had said to Martine Hayward.

She had opened the trunk of the car and he'd taken out Martine Hayward's black suitcase. Then they had all gone inside. Camille didn't like elevators, fearing they might get stuck between floors—a dream, or rather a nightmare, that she often had, she'd told him. And she was suspicious of the one that went up to the Auteuil apartment, an old-fashioned elevator, with two glass-paneled swing doors and very, very slow. On the landing in front of the apartment, she asked him:

"Are you coming in?"

"No, not tonight."

And when the aforementioned René-Marco opened the door, Bosmans heard the hubbub of conversations, and even made out a few silhouettes, in the living room in the rear. He took a step back and handed Martine Hayward's suitcase to Camille.

"Too bad you won't stay," Martine Hayward had said to him, giving his hand an insistent squeeze. "Some other evening, perhaps?"

And Deathmask had given him an ironic smile. The door had closed behind them and the aforementioned René-Marco. He had heaved a sigh of relief and hurtled down the stairs to finally breathe some fresh air. Night was falling and he walked aimlessly along the streets of Auteuil. He now regretted not visiting the house with them, for he could have questioned the woman in the black blouse—seemingly harmless questions, the answers to which might have told him something. If the aforementioned René-Marco knew Rose-Marie Krawell, did she frequent the apartment in Auteuil? He could easily see her moving about that living room among those people who were no more than outlines to him, but about whom Deathmask had hinted in a joking tone that most were meeting for the very first time and were not all entirely reputable.

He himself kept a rather hazy memory of Rose-Marie Krawell, a child's memory. In those days, she often spent a few days in the house on Rue du Docteur-Kurzenne and occupied the large bedroom on the second floor, which remained empty when she wasn't there. He wondered whether Martine Hayward could have met Rose-Marie Krawell. She had given him a peculiar look and answered curtly when he'd asked her, "Do you know the owner?"

All things considered, he shouldn't have left Camille and Martine Hayward just now, but rather tried to find out more about those people who met in the apartment, if only to learn their names.

He followed Rue Michel-Ange and went into a café where they were already stacking the chairs on the tables. He asked for a phone token and dialed the number of the "network" that Camille had given him: AUTEUIL 15-28, which she'd said was the apartment's old number. Men's and women's voices responded to one another: Blue Rider calling Alcibiades. 133 Avenue de Wagram, fourth floor. Paul will meet Henri this evening at Louis du Fiacre's place. Jacqueline and Sylvie are expecting you at the Marronniers, 27 Rue de Chazelles . . . Faraway voices, often muffled by static, which seemed to come from beyond the grave. After hanging up, he felt relieved to be back in the fresh air, as earlier when leaving the apartment building.

Perhaps he had just heard on the telephone, among the other voices and without recognizing it, the voice of Rose-Marie Krawell. For the first time in fifteen years, the woman's name occupied his mind, and that name would inevitably pull in its wake the memory of other individuals he'd seen with her, in the house on Rue du Docteur-Kurzenne. Up until then, his memories of those people had passed through a long period of hibernation;

but now it was finished, and the ghosts were not afraid to reappear in broad daylight. And who knew: over the coming years, they might return again and again, like blackmailers. Since he couldn't relive the past and correct it, the best way of rendering those ghosts harmless and keeping them at a distance would be to metamorphose them into characters in a novel.

That evening, he deemed Camille and Martine Hayward responsible for the return of those phantoms. Was their visit to the house on Rue du Docteur-Kurzenne merely a coincidence? There was certainly a connection, however tenuous, between them and the name Rose-Marie Krawell, spelled out plainly on the first page of a rental contract that also bore the name Martine Hayward. But none of this mattered much. And besides, when he was a child on Rue du Docteur-Kurzenne, he had never wondered about the people around him, had never tried to understand what he was doing there with them. On the contrary, it was they who should be wary of him after fifteen years. They might think he'd been some kind of witness, even a problematic one. And he remembered the title of an Italian film he'd seen at the Chaillot cinematheque: *The Children Are Watching Us*.

He hadn't noticed that he'd walked for almost forty-five minutes around Auteuil, up to one of the limits of that neighborhood, running along the Seine, and that he'd retraced his steps. It was now dark. He followed a narrow street, right near that René-Marco's apartment to whose door he'd accompanied Camille and Martine Hayward. He wondered whether he should take the elevator with its glass-paneled swing doors, which rose so slowly that Camille was afraid it would stall between floors. He wanted to get to the bottom of this: was AUTEUIL 15-28 really a disused number, as Camille had claimed, or still the number for the apartment? And did certain voices he'd heard after dialing AUTEUIL 15-28, voices that sounded as if from beyond the grave, belong to people he'd seen in the living room? The first time Camille had brought him there, he might have met Rose-Marie Krawell, but would they have recognized each other after fifteen years? Ten o'clock, the hour when those ghosts came together on the wide, low sofas of the living room.

Early one afternoon, Bosmans decided to ring at the door of the apartment. If he wanted to clarify matters—the expression had occurred to him when he'd accompanied Camille aka Deathmask and Martine Hayward to the house on Rue du Docteur-Kurzenne—he needed to see what the apartment looked like in broad daylight, and not after dark among the anonymous shadows he'd rubbed shoulders with in the living room.

It was, in fact, a sunny afternoon, and in the April light the outlines of passersby, the leaves on the trees, the sidewalks and building façades stood out sharply under the blue sky, as if they'd been pressure-washed to remove every last trace of dust or blurriness. He took the elevator, which he'd not yet done because of Camille. Bosmans sat on the red velvet bench and would have liked that slow, gentle rise to continue indefinitely. Then he would have closed his eyes and felt no more anxiety.

He rang three times, with some apprehension. At that time of day, there was probably no one home. Nothing disturbed the silence. It even seemed like the entire building was deserted. He rang three more times. Then he heard the sound of footsteps. The door opened onto the girl he'd seen one evening walking away down the hall, holding the little boy's hand, on his first visit, and with whom he'd crossed paths another time at the entrance with the same little boy. Deathmask had told him, "That's René-Marco's son and the au pair."

"I think I've come much too early." And he spoke that sentence, which he'd prepared just in case, prior to ringing, in a blank voice.

But she showed no surprise. She closed the door behind them and led him into the living room, as if it were the waiting room of a doctor or dentist.

"Please have a seat."

She indicated one of the large sofas and sat down beside him. A stack of magazines was on the sofa, one of them open.

"I was reading while the little one takes his nap."

She'd said it matter-of-factly. Had she guessed that he knew about the child's existence?

"In the evening and at night, don't the guests make too much noise?"

"Oh, no, not at all. The hall between the living room and our bedroom is long. The boy always sleeps soundly."

She had answered in a calm voice, looking him in the eye.

"That's a relief."

She smiled slightly. She must have been his age, about twenty. She seemed neither surprised by his presence nor curious to know why he'd rung at the door of the apartment so early in the afternoon.

"I came by on the off-chance. I was hoping to catch Mr. René-Marco to ask him something."

Since he didn't know the man's last name, he felt obliged to say "Mr. René-Marco."

"Do you mean Mr. Heriford?"

She suddenly displayed the solicitousness of a schoolteacher correcting a pupil's grammar mistake. And because of her age, it gave her a certain charm.

"Yes, of course, I mean Mr. René-Marco Heriford."

He glanced around him. The room was not at all the same as the one in the evening and at night. A large, bright room with couches in soft colors, the window half open on the leaves of a chestnut tree, a splash of sunlight on the back wall, and this young woman, sitting beside him, bust straight and arms folded. He must have gotten off at the wrong floor.

"Mr. Heriford always comes home very late. During the day, I'm here alone with the child."

"René-Marco Heriford's son?"

He couldn't keep from saying the man's full name, to be sure there was no ambiguity about who he meant.

"Exactly."

"And have you worked here long?"

"Two years."

She didn't seem thrown by any question, even from a stranger.

"I tried calling before I stopped by, but the phone didn't answer."

He felt ashamed about lying to her, but it was just a white lie.

"What number did you use?"

"AUTEUIL 15-28."

"Oh, no. The numbers have gone to seven digits now."

She looked at him in puzzlement. Clearly, she took him for an oddball.

"I'll give you the correct number later, if you'd like."

Given all this goodwill, he thought he might ask some more questions.

"And . . . do you know most of the people who come here at night?"

This time, she showed some hesitation about answering.

"It's none of my business."

She forced herself to add:

"If you ask me, they're probably contacts of Mr. Heriford's."

What did she mean by "contacts"?

"But you, aren't you a friend of Mr. Heriford's?"

She seemed to have some doubt about that. Perhaps because this Mr. Heriford was not the same age as Bosmans. On the rare evenings when Deathmask had brought him to this room, the people he'd met were also older than he.

"A friend of mine introduced me to Mr. Heriford. Camille Lucas. Do you know her?"

"No, I don't believe so."

"And a friend of Camille Lucas's who comes here often: Martine Hayward?"

"I've sometimes come across a few people in the evenings, when making the boy's dinner. But I don't know their names. I'll tell Mr. Heriford you came by, if I see him this evening."

There was a moment of silence between them. Perhaps she was waiting for him to take his leave. He looked for words to gain time.

"How late does the little one nap?"

"Until three-thirty. Afterward, I often take him for his afternoon snack at the Ferme d'Auteuil."

The Ferme d'Auteuil. That place, near the racetrack, brought back a childhood memory. An outdoor restaurant beneath the trees. At the back of a garden, a shed that housed several cows. And, farther on, a pony. In his memory, the Ferme d'Auteuil was very close to the Vallée de Chevreuse, Rue du Docteur-Kurzenne, and the no-man's-land around Porte Molitor where he was born. It all formed a secret province. And no Geological Survey map or street guide to Paris could have convinced him otherwise.

"You're right . . . The Ferme d'Auteuil is a good idea."

"And what about you, do you live around here?"

He didn't know whether she'd asked out of politeness or curiosity.

"Yes. Right nearby. I walked over."

He was lying, but as of tomorrow he'd look for a room to rent in the neighborhood.

"And Mr. Heriford, has he lived here long?"

She hesitated in answering.

"I think a friend of his is lending him the apartment."

Should he keep asking questions? She'd end up getting suspicious. But then again, sometimes you have to take risks.

"And what about the boy's mother?"

Clearly, that question had crossed a line.

After a moment of awkwardness, she said, lowering her eyes:

"I don't know . . . I've never seen her. Mr. Heriford has never mentioned her to me . . . "

He tried to think of something to break the discomfort. He rested his hand on the pile of magazines between them.

"Do you read all these magazines?"

But she hadn't heard him. Her mind was elsewhere.

"I don't dare ask about his wife . . . I get the impression she's dead . . . "

It was as if she was talking to herself and had forgotten his presence. Then she turned to him.

"You can stay a bit longer . . . The little boy doesn't get up until three-thirty . . . "

No doubt she preferred not to be alone. For her it must have been like this every morning and every afternoon in that empty apartment. One of the windows was open a crack, but no cars were passing in the street. And the silence was so profound that you could hear the leaves rustling. The people who got together in late evening left the apartment at what they call the break of day. And, after that, only she and the child remained behind in the back room.

"Yes, of course . . . I have plenty of time . . . and it would be a pleasure to keep you company."

These phrases, which he had blurted out, were somewhat solemn and precious, like the final lines of a scene in a play or the last verse of a recited poem. But no, apparently they hadn't surprised her. Moreover, she answered in the same tone:

"That's very kind of you . . . And I'm grateful . . . "

She looked at her watch.

"Just another ten minutes or so. Anyway, if he's still asleep, I'll go wake him . . . "

And then, as every day, she and the boy would leave the apartment and walk to the Ferme d'Auteuil. On the living room wall, the blotch of sunlight had moved to the right, and he noticed another in the middle of the sofa, next to them. No, he had surely gotten off at the wrong floor. This couldn't be the same room into which Deathmask had pulled him two or three times, and where he tried to follow the conversations around him without understanding a single word. And, as the night progressed, the music playing softly in the background became louder and louder, and the light got lower and lower, until the living room was nearly in darkness. Then it was no longer time for conversation. Shadows blended with one another on the sofas, and the music covered their sighs and whispers. And, each time, he had taken advantage of the dark to slip through the half-open living room door into the vestibule, leaving behind him Camille aka Deathmask and Martine Hayward amid all those shadows interlaced on the sofas.

"A penny for your thoughts."

She had said this in a friendly, detached tone. He didn't know what to answer. He stared at the spot of sunlight on the couch.

"I feel like I got off at the wrong floor."

But he could see from her eyes and knitted brow that she didn't understand what he meant.

"This apartment isn't at all the same as at night. If you hadn't mentioned René-Marco Heriford, I would have thought I'd come to the wrong place."

She had listened very attentively, like a good pupil trying to follow a complex math lesson. And then she remained silent a moment, brows still knit, as if reflecting on every word he'd just pronounced.

"I don't have the same impression as you . . . Whatever happens here at night doesn't concern me. And I don't try to find out anything about Mr. Heriford's guests. They just hired me to take care of the child. Do you understand?"

She had said it so firmly that it felt like a bucket of cold water someone might splash in your face to wake you up. He wondered whether he had ever really been in this apartment at night or whether it was just a bad dream, the kind that recurs regularly. Each time, as you're falling asleep, you're afraid you might have it again, and the dream is so insistent that all the next day you retain scraps of it, unable to disentangle day from night. And yet, Deathmask had indeed dragged him to this living room amid all those shadows. But he ended up doubting whether Deathmask and Martine Hayward really existed.

"I completely understand what you said and I think you're right."

He could almost have thanked her for pulling him out of a nightmare. He was convinced that, if he stayed with her in this living room until the end of the afternoon and later into the evening, no one would come to the door of the apartment, not Deathmask, not Martine Hayward. Not even Rose-Marie Krawell or any other ghost.

She looked at her watch.

"It's twenty to four, I have to go wake up the boy . . . But first I have to make a phone call . . . Will you excuse me?"

She got up, gave him a broad smile, and through the half-open double-door slipped into the bathroom that was off the living room, something he'd noticed that first evening when Deathmask had brought him here.

He could hear her talking on the phone, very faintly, and he supposed she was in a bedroom several rooms away from the bathroom. The arrangement of rooms in this place struck him as odd, but perhaps he was imagining things and it was a perfectly ordinary apartment, the kind found by the hundreds in this residential neighborhood.

She returned after a few minutes.

"It was for the boy. I called Dr. Rouveix . . . We finally decided he should come here in a little while to give the boy his vaccine . . . "

She had said it with a kind of professional seriousness, as if he knew this Dr. Rouveix.

"It's very handy . . . Dr. Rouveix lives just down the street and always comes over for the boy."

He thought he should leave before Dr. Rouveix arrived.

He stood up.

"And I guess after that you'll take the boy to the Ferme d'Auteuil?"

"I don't know. I'll ask Dr. Rouveix if it's better for him to stay here after his shot."

She walked him to the front door.

"Let me give you the current phone number," she said with a hint of a smile. "The one with seven digits . . . "

She handed him a sheet of paper folded in four.

"You can call in the morning or early afternoon. I'm always here."

She seemed to hesitate for a moment. Then, in a lower voice:

"But don't call AUTEUIL 15-28 in the evening. You're liable to come across some unsavory individuals."

She gave a brief laugh.

On the landing, the elevator seemed to be waiting, as if no one had used it since he'd arrived earlier that afternoon. Before shutting the apartment door, she gave him a very slight wave.

In the street, he unfolded the sheet she'd handed him. Written on it was: Kim, 288-15-28.

Strange first name. But it had something pert and cheerful about it, like the little crystalline signal the conductor of the old platform buses used to sound, giving the chain a sharp jerk to announce the departure. Moreover, the sun and freshness of the air were as springlike as at the start of the afternoon. Only one detail bothered him: the apartment's new phone number was indeed seven digits, but it still had the same four last numbers as the old one: AUTEUIL 15-28. Still, he was certain he wouldn't hear those voices from the afterworld if he dialed 288-15-28. It had only taken a lovely spring day.

Approaching the end of Rue Michel-Ange, he crossed paths with a dark-haired man, with a tanned face, short hair, and athletic bearing, who was carrying a leather bag with a slight rocking motion. Their eyes met, and he was tempted to speak to him. It might have been Dr. Rouveix. He turned around and watched him walk with a regular gait. He would have liked to follow him to verify whether he was in fact heading toward the apartment building, but he considered that pointless and indiscreet. The next time he called 288-15-28, he'd give Kim a physical description of the man and ask if it was indeed Dr. Rouveix.

He felt light as he walked that afternoon, wandering aimlessly in the streets of Auteuil. He thought about that apartment, so different by day and by night, as if belonging to two parallel worlds. But why should that bother him? For years he'd been used to living in the narrow margin between reality and dream, letting them illuminate each other, sometimes blend together, while he continued on his way with a decided step, not deviating by a centimeter, which he knew would have upset a precarious balance. On more than one occasion, he'd been called a sleepwalker, and to a certain degree the word had seemed a compliment. Once upon a time, people used to consult sleepwalkers for their gift of second sight. He felt no different from them. What mattered was not to slip off the ridgeline and to know just how far one can dream one's life.

He would gladly have walked to the Ferme d'Auteuil to see whether it matched his recollections. The place had surely changed in fifteen years, lost its rustic appearance. As he drew closer to the area around the racetracks, he remembered coming there once, to that Ferme d'Auteuil, with Rose-Marie Krawell and a rather tall dark-haired man whom he wouldn't have been able to recognize even if someone had shown him a photo of the fellow at the time. The only detail he could have furnished about that faceless man was the watch he wore on his wrist, a huge watch whose multiple faces, of different sizes, marked the days, months, and years, and even the different phases of the moon. The man had explained all this to him while handing him the watch and letting him wear it for a moment. And he had specified that this was an "American army watch," three words whose sound had been more important to him than the exact meaning, since they still resounded in his memory with a muffled echo.

At the Ferme d'Auteuil that afternoon, Rose-Marie Krawell had sat facing him. He wondered whether he'd be able to recognize *her* after fifteen years. A blonde with large light-colored eyes. Cropped hair. Average height. Wearing bracelets with large links. Those were the vague terms he would have used to describe her. On top of which, he retained a few impressions. Her deep voice. Her slightly brusque way of speaking. Her cigarette lighter, which she took from her handbag and gave him to play with. The lighter had her scent.

Leaving the Ferme d'Auteuil, the three of them, Rose-Marie Krawell, the dark-haired man, and he, had gotten into a black car. Rose-Marie Krawell was at the wheel, the man next to her, and he in the back seat. And they had ended up in an apartment near the Ferme d'Auteuil, as the drive seemed short. But when it comes to childhood memories, you have to take anything about distance or the time spent getting from one place to another with a grain of salt, as well as about the order of events you believe occurred in the same afternoon, when in fact they occurred weeks or years apart.

In one bedroom of the apartment, Rose-Marie Krawell was sitting on the corner of a desk and talking on the telephone. She had taken back her lighter, which she had lent him to play with, and with that scented lighter she lit a cigarette. The man with the "American army watch" sat near him on a couch and showed how you get the watch to make a little alarm sound, at the time when you want to wake up. You only had to stop the blue needle on the number of the hour in question and push a button at the bottom of the dial. But apart from those specific movements, he remembered no details from that day, as if he were studying under a loupe the only remaining scrap of a torn photograph.

He had reached the boulevard, not far from the racetracks. On the spur of the moment, he decided not to cross the street to go to the Ferme d'Auteuil. He no longer felt like making such a pilgrimage alone. He remembered that on the face of the "American army watch," you could make the hands turn backward simply by pressing. If he crossed the threshold of the Ferme d'Auteuil today and sat at one of the tables, in the garden, he would go back through time. He would find himself at the same table with Rose-Marie Krawell and the man with the "American army watch." He'd be his current age, but they would be exactly the same as fifteen years ago. They wouldn't have aged a day. And he could finally ask them some precise questions. Would they be able to answer? Would they want to?

If fifteen years had already seemed, back then, too long a time to prevent his childhood recollections from getting muddled, what could he say now? Nearly fifty years had passed since that car ride with Camille and Martine Hayward through the Vallée de Chevreuse and to the house on Rue du Docteur-Kurzenne. Yes, nearly fifty years since the first afternoon he'd spent with Kim in the living room of the Auteuil apartment, where he had crossed paths with Dr. Rouveix—for it had indeed been he—on a prematurely springlike day in a year he wished he could identify. Spring of '64 or '65? The two blended together in his memory, and he lacked the specific reference points to tell them apart.

In what circumstances had he met Camille aka Deathmask? He hadn't asked himself that question in fifty years. Little by little, time had erased the different periods of his life, none of which had a connection with the subsequent one, and as such that life had been only a series of interruptions, avalanches, or even amnesias.

So where *had* he first met Camille? After straining his memory, a hazy image appeared to him. Camille, sitting in a café at a table next to his—on a winter's day, as the silhouettes around them were wearing overcoats. And he concluded that it could only have been in the restaurant in Place Blanche, on the ground floor. He in fact saw himself, that day, crossing the street with Camille and accompanying her to the Place Blanche pharmacy. There were a few customers ahead of her and she seemed nervous. She was clutching a prescription. She explained in a murmur that she wasn't sure they'd give her the medicine, as the prescription was a year old. But when she handed the slip to one of the pharmacists, he went to the back of the shop and returned with a small pink box without any comment, a small pink box that Bosmans later noticed she always carried in her handbag and placed on the nightstand. So it is that one recovers apparently insignificant details, which had been hibernating in the night of time. He remembered the thick coating of snow on Paris that winter, into which their shoes sank. And the patches of black ice.

She lived a bit lower down from Place Blanche, in a room on a street with a sharp bend whose name he'd forgotten. One detail had struck him from the start. Her name was Camille Lucas, but one evening while waiting for her in her room, he had discovered a passport in which was written: Gaul, Camille Jeannette, née Lucas, born Nantes, 16 September 1943. He had asked her about that "Gaul." She'd shrugged.

"I got married too young . . . I haven't seen my husband in almost three years . . . "

She worked in an office. He had gone to pick her up several times, on the second floor of one of those buildings facing the Gare Saint-Lazare on which luminous advertisements shine at night, their multicolored letters parading without end. What kind of office was it? She'd said it was an accounting firm. She pronounced the word "accounting" very gravely. She had "studied accounting," and he had never dared ask her what, exactly, that consisted of.

She was glad to have found this job at Saint-Lazare and to have left her previous employ, another "accounting" position in a hotel-restaurant, a little farther up on Rue de La Rochefoucauld.

One detail in his memory sometimes carried along others, agglutinated to the first, the way currents carry rotting clumps of algae. And besides, topology sometimes helps you awaken the most distant recollections. He now saw himself with Deathmask in a café around Saint-Lazare, on the same block as her office building, one of those cafés too close to the station for the customers to take their time. They gulped down their drinks at the bar before letting themselves be swept away and getting lost in the rush-hour crowds. That café was also like a border post of the neighboring 8th arrondissement. At the back of the main room, the picture window looked out on a quiet street. If you were to follow that street to the end, you would leave behind the crowds and cesspool of Saint-Lazare and end up in the leafy shade of the gardens on the Champs-Elysées.

At the rear table, in fact, right near the picture window, Bosmans had occasionally sat with Camille and a friend of hers, the only one she'd kept from among her "colleagues," as she called them, from her previous employ.

This was a certain Michel de Gama. The name had stuck in his memory, as he had later asked himself many questions about the man who bore it. Camille had met him when she worked in the hotel-restaurant on Rue de La Rochefoucauld. He was somehow associated with "the boss," and they often talked about other people, "colleagues" or patrons of that Hotel Chatham.

Michel de Gama was older than they were. Brown hair swept back and too meticulously dressed, with dark suits and ties in matching hues. According to Deathmask, his mother was French, and his father had worked "in a Latin American embassy." He himself spoke a slightly odd French, sometimes with an indefinable accent, sometimes with distinctly Parisian intonations and slang expressions. And when you listened to him, that dissonance caused a vague unease.

In the café at Saint-Lazare, Michel de Gama seemed to be hiding out; the many customers huddled around the bar rendered him invisible, sitting all the way in back, far from the general agitation and hubbub. To the left of his table, a small glass-paneled door opened onto a quiet street that must have been Rue d'Anjou, Rue de l'Arcade, or Rue Pasquier. He always entered the café via the glass-paneled door, the way someone might sneak into a movie theater through the emergency exit. And the slight unease you felt in his presence also came from the fact that, even though he spoke volubly and with a certain self-assurance, he always seemed on his guard, as if expecting an imminent police raid.

Bosmans had asked Camille why she still saw this Michel de Gama, since her memories of the people she'd known at the hotel-restaurant on Rue de La Rochefoucauld were mostly unpleasant. She had answered evasively: "I wouldn't want to get on his bad side." He clearly inspired some fear in her. As he was always in the neighborhood, she risked running into him as she left work, or farther up the street, where she lived.

She confessed that she preferred not to be alone with Michel de Gama, and she always asked Bosmans to accompany her to their appointments. One afternoon at around five, he was sitting at their usual table, at the back of the café, between Camille and Michel de Gama. He noticed that the latter was wearing a signet ring on his left hand, its stone engraved with a coat of arms. And, no doubt because of that ring, he asked in a vaguely sarcastic tone:

"Are you related to the explorer Vasco de Gama?"

The other gave him a hard look and remained silent, the kind of silence that portends danger. Camille had also noticed it and seemed nervous.

"Did you hear me? I asked if you're related to the explorer Vasco de Gama."

Normally so gentle and affable, he could sometimes turn insolent with someone toward whom he felt antipathy.

But suddenly the hard look clouded over and Michel de Gama gave him a wide grin, though the grin seemed forced.

"I see you're interested in my family history. Unfortunately, I cannot give you much information."

He'd spoken those words with the foreign accent he occasionally adopted, which sounded like an affectation. And his eyes locked onto Bosmans as if to drive home that it really was time to change the subject.

"No harm meant," Camille had said with a shrug. "Jean is very interested in genealogy and family names."

The three of them had left via the small glass-paneled door. On the sidewalk, before taking his leave, Michel de Gama shook his hand.

"You know," he'd said, "in life, it's best not to be too curious."

Another smile, but with nothing friendly about it, owing to the cold gaze fixed on Bosmans.

De Gama headed off down Rue de l'Arcade, unless it was Rue Pasquier, or d'Anjou. The two of them stood there, silent, as if waiting until he was out of sight.

Camille was pensive.

"You have to be careful with him. He can be a bit sensitive."

And she explained, without spelling it out, that while Michel de Gama and the few individuals she had known on Rue de La Rochefoucauld, in that Hotel Chatham, had always been very nice to her, they "didn't really like people asking questions." And yet, "from an accounting standpoint," everything seemed "above board," even "impeccable," at the Hotel Chatham.

He didn't understand exactly who these people were, and Camille's explanations were not very clear. He realized she was afraid of saying too much. So: there was this manager of the Hotel Chatham, of whom Michel de Gama was an associate, and two friends of theirs who ran the restaurant. And a few other friends, patrons of the hotel and the restaurant. This formed a "group" of about a dozen. He had to wait many years before knowing more about the Hotel Chatham and the "group" that Camille had alluded to, a rather dubious circle of individuals. But that new perspective changed nothing about his memories of that time in his life. On the contrary, it confirmed certain of his impressions, and he rediscovered them intact and strong as ever, as if time had been abolished. Back then, he had constantly walked throughout Paris, and everything was bathed in a light that lent a vivid phosphorescence to the people and streets. Then, as he got older, he noticed that this light had slowly dimmed; it now showed people and things as they were, in their true colors—the lackluster colors of everyday life. He told himself that his attention as a nocturnal spectator had also diminished. But it might just be that after so many years, this world and those streets had changed, and no longer evoked anything for him.

He accompanied Camille to her appointments with Michel de Gama at Saint-Lazare two or three more times. The latter seemed to have forgotten, or forgiven, the question about his family name, and showed him a surface amiability. At the last of these appointments in the café, as he was taking his leave, Michel de Gama had said to Camille, pointing to him:

"You really should bring him to have dinner with us some evening at the Chatham."

Camille maintained an awkward silence. Michel de Gama turned to him:

"I'm curious to know what you'll make of the Chatham . . . I'm certain you'll find the place interesting."

"Yes, but he's not used to staying out late in that kind of establishment," Camille had said in a sharp voice, as if to protect him.

"Well, then, just come for a drink," Michel de Gama had said.

"Gladly."

Camille seemed taken aback by his reply. But he had considered the invitation unimportant. He felt sorry about ruffling the man's feathers the other day by bringing up Vasco de Gama, without really understanding why he'd gotten into a huff over so little.

"Both of you come tomorrow at seven."

He headed off down the street, erect in his dark suit. He wasn't wearing a coat despite the cold, probably out of vanity.

"You shouldn't have accepted," Camille said. "He's a pretty disreputable character."

Whether this "character" was reputable or not didn't matter to Bosmans. What could he fear from him? And first of all, was his name really Michel de Gama? He'd wondered that from the start. If a man doesn't use his real name, it's because he has doubts about himself. On top of which, in the café at Saint-Lazare, he always sat with his back to the wall and cast anxious glances at the passing customers, over there, at the bar, as if he didn't feel entirely safe. "I'm curious to know what you'll make of the Chatham," he'd said. And he, Bosmans, was curious to observe how Michel de Gama acted in that environment.

One of those calm streets, before reaching the fringes of Pigalle and Place Blanche, in the area he called "the first slopes." The hotel's façade and entrance didn't stand out from the neighboring buildings. The restaurant dining room opened onto the sidewalk. At the hotel entrance, an oval plaque in black marble bore the inscription in gold letters: HOTEL CHATHAM.

Camille had stopped before the door, looking uneasy.

"It feels strange to come back here . . . "

Michel de Gama was waiting for them in a kind of small lounge, to the left of the reception, with a white marble mantelpiece on which sat an antique pendulum clock. A few engravings on the walls depicted hunting scenes. In a corner of the room was a dark wood bar. It looked like a provincial inn.

He seemed more relaxed than in the café at Saint-Lazare. He motioned for them to have a seat on the settee near the bar. Then he went over to the bar and poured three glasses of a liqueur that, given the shape of the bottle, must have been port.

He took a seat facing them. He gave Bosmans a quizzical stare, as if waiting for him to come out with an appraisal of the hotel. Bosmans had to say something quickly.

"It's very peaceful here . . . "

He regretted not finding other words. But to his relief, Michel de Gama's face broke out into a smile.

"That's exactly what my associate Guy Vincent and I were hoping to create," he said, this time with his slight foreign accent. "Something peaceful, simple, and classic."

And he held out his glass so the three of them could toast.

"Camille could take you to see her old office."

"Oh, no . . . I'd rather not."

She had said it in a gentle voice, as if in apology and so as not to offend Michel de Gama.

"It's really my associate Guy Vincent's office. He's often away from Paris and he lent it to Camille."

She nodded, like someone waiting for something to end. Bosmans was afraid she might stand up suddenly and drag him outside.

"We have a regular clientele. And often friends of ours. It kind of makes for a small club."

He had forced his foreign accent, in which you could now discern British intonations. For his way of speaking, and the cut of his suit, he had surely taken someone elegant and admired as his model.

"There's never anyone here before dinnertime," Michel de Gama said abruptly, no doubt to justify the silence in the hotel. "This is the quiet hour . . . The blue hour, as my associate Guy Vincent would say."

It was the third time Bosmans heard him speak the phrase "my associate Guy Vincent." The name Guy Vincent was not unknown to him. But at that moment, if someone had asked him point blank, he wouldn't have been able to say precisely what it evoked. Maybe he was merely struck by the sound of it.

Michel de Gama no longer had the anxious look he wore at Saint-Lazare. He seemed at ease in the bar, or rather the lounge, of this hotel, as if he were at home here and enjoyed a kind of diplomatic immunity between these walls. No doubt it ceased the minute he set foot in the street. What exactly was his situation? Persona non grata in Paris? Bosmans would have loved to ask.

"I'll have to show you the rooms."

This time, he regained his Paris accent.

"Not tonight," Camille said curtly. "Anyway, we'll come again."

But this was clearly an empty promise.

"Camille sometimes used to stay in one of the rooms," Michel de Gama said, turning toward him.

"Only on days when I had too much work and had to be up very early."

There was a hint of exasperation in her voice.

Michel de Gama took a pack of English cigarettes from his pocket and lit one with a lighter. He had to flick it several times before the flame shot up, a tall flame that startled Bosmans. And when he snapped the lighter shut, the sharp click reminded Bosmans of something.

"That's a very handsome lighter." And Bosmans felt as if that sentence had been spoken by a double of himself.

"It produces a good flame . . . Care to try it?"

Michel de Gama handed him the lighter. Scarcely had he grasped it between his thumb and index than he relived an old sensation. It was confirmed when the flame shot up again, a flame that was unexpectedly high, given the lighter's diminutive size. The sensation suddenly cast him fifteen years in the past, and the shock was as unexpected as that of the bumper cars of his childhood. In a flash, he saw Rose-Marie Krawell hand him the same lighter, telling him to be careful of the flame.

"Yes, a very handsome lighter. But you have to be careful of the flame."

He had handed the lighter back to Michel de Gama; the latter stared at him curiously, as Bosmans must have looked strange when repeating that sentence from so far in the past.

"At least show him your old office," said Michel de Gama, turning to Camille.

She stood up silently. She had taken Bosmans's arm and they followed a long corridor lit at the ceiling by what seemed to be night-lights.

"I'll show you the office, and then we'll tell him we have to leave," she said under her breath.

She opened a door on which was attached a small gold plate with a number that must originally have been the number of one of the hotel rooms. Light fell dimly from a ceiling fixture. A desk of blond wood in the middle of the room and, in the corner, a very narrow sofa. The window looked out onto the courtyard.

"This is where you did your accounting?"

There was no sarcasm in his voice, only a kind of gravity.

"Yes. This is it."

He walked over to the desk and sat in the leather chair behind it. Numerous drawers on both sides.

"So this was Guy Vincent's desk?"

She nodded, but as if she was thinking of something else, perhaps about leaving this room as quickly as possible. He, too, was lost in thought. The flame of the lighter Michel de Gama had handed him had been a revelation. That flame lit a dark room, and the name Guy Vincent, after a long period of amnesia, had again become familiar to him.

And indeed, there was a photo on the right-hand corner of the desk, in a garnet leather frame, and, leaning toward it, he recognized Guy Vincent with his hand on a woman's shoulder, his wife—a woman whose first name he remembered: Gaëlle. But she came less often than he to the house on Rue du Docteur-Kurzenne. Bosmans remembered her only in broad daylight. She had never slept at the house. When Guy Vincent came alone, he occupied the large upstairs bedroom. Bosmans easily recognized him in the photo: short hair, tall, light-colored eyes. In those days, he'd thought Guy Vincent was "American," because of his build and his convertible car, and also because he'd heard someone say he'd spent a long time in America. And yet he had a French name. He suddenly recalled something Guy Vincent said, one afternoon when the latter had asked him to go check the mail in the box on Rue du Docteur-Kurzenne. And in fact, he had found a letter on whose envelope was written "Roger Vincent," with the address of the house. When he'd handed over the letter, Guy Vincent had said,

"You know, I like to change my first name now and then," as if he were owed an explanation.

Camille was standing before him, watching him in silence. His eyes met hers. Did she suspect something? She knew almost nothing about him, he'd never talked to her about what his life had been like before they met, and he especially never would have had the ludicrous idea of relating his childhood memories. Besides, he felt as if only the present moment interested her.

He opened the drawers on both sides of the desk, one by one, to see what they contained, and that made Camille smile.

"So, are you executing a search warrant?"

She'd said it in a mocking tone, and the term "search warrant" made him feel uneasy. Why had she chosen that phrase?

The left-hand drawers were empty. So were the three top ones on the right. But the bottom drawer held three sheets of letterhead and a book bound in green leather.

Camille sat on the narrow sofa with her back against the wall. She kept watching him, a smile on her lips. There were indeed three sheets of letterhead, blank and a bit yellowed by time, at the top of which was printed in debossed letters: "Guy Vincent, 12 Rue Nicolas-Chuquet, Paris XVII." And the green leatherbound volume was a datebook, but for some reason the page indicating the year was missing.

He folded the sheets in four and slid them into his inside jacket pocket, along with the datebook. The photo in the leather frame was too big for him to hide in another pocket. Camille had noticed his hesitation. She pointed to her handbag, which was almost as large as a suitcase. He stuffed the photo in it.

"Do you know Guy Vincent?" he asked.

"I only saw him once, when I first started working here. He's rarely in Paris."

Her voice was calm, indifferent. She had manifested no surprise watching him steal the letterhead, datebook, and photo.

"You wouldn't know how Michel de Gama met Guy Vincent, would you?"

She didn't seem the least bit surprised by the question.

"Gosh, I don't know . . . "

She had shrugged. Such indifference and nonchalance suddenly struck him as suspicious, and he remembered the term "search warrant" that she'd used when watching him rifle through the desk drawers.

"Did they meet in prison?"

He had asked the question suddenly. If she knew more about Guy Vincent than she let on, this might be a way to get her to talk. But she kept smiling, as if she hadn't heard.

"You should ask him yourself . . . "

And the reply had been spoken in the tone of some-one giving you a piece of friendly advice—with all due humility.

They rejoined Michel de Gama, who was just ending a phone conversation, alone at the reception desk.

"So did she show you the office of my associate Guy Vincent?"

He too was smiling, but with a different smile than Camille's, a slightly forced smile, as if something was worrying him. Perhaps what his interlocutor had just told him over the phone. All of a sudden, Bosmans imag-ined that Michel de Gama had come to join them in the office of "his associate Guy Vincent," and that he was just about to open the door when he'd overheard what they were saying, especially the phrase said a bit too loudly: "Did they meet in prison?" And he immediately regret-ted saying such a thing and losing his composure.

"I was especially interested in seeing where Camille used to work."

This time, he'd made an effort to sound like a pleas-ant young man.

"She could work there still . . . We were all very sorry she decided to leave us."

Bosmans would have liked to know whether this "we" included Guy Vincent.

"Isn't that right, Camille? We were totally unprepared for your departure."

She spread her arms shyly, in a sign of powerlessness, and she, too, looked just like a naïve young girl.

"It's getting late," she said, holding out her hand to Michel de Gama. "We should be going."

He accompanied them to the front door of the hotel and stopped at the threshold. Bosmans's thought from earlier ran through his mind: this man couldn't set foot outside because he was persona non grata.

"I like your hotel very much," he said to Michel de Gama. "People must feel at peace here, which is becoming increasingly rare in Paris."

But he felt that was insufficient and added:

"Bravo to you and your associate."

Michel de Gama's smile softened.

"He would have been so happy to hear you say that."

They shook hands, and Bosmans was overcome by dizziness. It would have taken only a few sentences to tip into the void: "Please give him my best . . . Perhaps your associate remembers me . . . From the time when he liked changing names."

"I hope we'll see each other again soon," Michel de Gama said to him. "As soon as possible."

He felt relieved to walk steadily on the sidewalk and to have resisted that spell. Camille took from her handbag the photograph of Guy Vincent and his wife in its leather frame.

"Here . . . before I forget . . . "

She didn't seem to want to know why he'd stolen the

photo, datebook, and sheets of letterhead. And what if Michel de Gama were to notice? Apparently, that hadn't occurred to her either. He had gotten used to her nonchalance, but even so, he was surprised by her lack of curiosity about this. He told himself that, all in all, if that Guy Vincent was linked to certain childhood memories of his, it was no business of hers and of absolutely no concern.

It was impossible for Bosmans, after more than fifty years, to establish the precise chronology of those two past events: crossing the Vallée de Chevreuse in a car with Camille and Martine Hayward, which landed them in front of the house on Rue du Docteur-Kurzenne; and visiting the Hotel Chatham, where he and Camille found themselves in the office of Guy Vincent.

All the reference markers had faded with time, so that these two events, seen from so great a distance, appeared contemporaneous, and even ended up blending into one another, like a double-exposed photograph.

A coincidence troubled him. By what happenstance had Camille and Martine Hayward brought him back, twice, to a period of his childhood that he hadn't thought about in fifteen years? It was as if they'd done it deliberately, for an unknown reason, and that someone had informed them about certain details of his early life.

Camille had worked as an accountant at the Hotel Chatham in Guy Vincent's office, and Martine Hayward had rented the house on Rue du Docteur-Kurzenne, which still belonged back then to Rose-Marie Krawell. And among the notes he'd taken to try to put some order into all this figured the answer Camille had given him when he'd asked if Martine Hayward knew the owner of the house: "I think René-Marco knows her."

He had appended to his notes a kind of schema, as if to guide himself through a labyrinth:

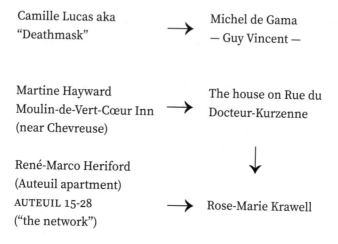

Camille Lucas aka "Deathmask" → Michel de Gama — Guy Vincent —

Martine Hayward Moulin-de-Vert-Cœur Inn (near Chevreuse) → The house on Rue du Docteur-Kurzenne

René-Marco Heriford (Auteuil apartment) AUTEUIL 15-28 ("the network") → Rose-Marie Krawell

And he resolved to complete this schema as other names recurred in his memory, or as he discovered them in the course of his research—names related to the ones he had exhumed from oblivion. And perhaps he'd manage to establish an overall plan.

It was a difficult but instructive exercise. At first you think you've chanced upon coincidences, but after fifty years you have a panoramic view of your life. And you tell yourself that if you dug deeply, like those archeologists who end up bringing to light an entire buried city and its tangle of streets, you'd be amazed to discover connections with people whose existence you hadn't suspected or that you'd forgotten, a network around you that expanded into infinity.

These lofty reflections could not ward off a feeling of unease that he tried to conquer by telling himself his imagination was playing tricks on him. At certain moments of the day, he laughed at himself and drew up a list of novel titles that translated his state of mind:

—*The Return of the Ghosts*
—*The Mysteries of the Hotel Chatham*
—*The Haunted House on Rue du Docteur-Kurzenne*
—*Auteuil 15-28*
—*Meetings at Saint-Lazare*
—*The Office of Guy Vincent*
—*The Secret Life of René-Marco Heriford*

But at night, in his hours of insomnia, he no longer felt like laughing. He was convinced that all those people—even Camille—were aware of the slightest details of his childhood, and especially of that long period when he'd lived in the house on Rue du Docteur-Kurzenne. And their circle, fifteen years later, had tightened around him. A game of cat and mouse, the reasons for which he tried to fathom.

The second time he visited the Auteuil apartment in early afternoon, the door of the concierge's lodge was ajar, and he would have liked to ask the man a few questions. He was certainly aware of the movements of the people who went upstairs to the apartment in evening and nighttime and came back down at daybreak; the other building residents must have remarked on it. But he preferred not to risk being seen.

He had gone up in the elevator with the glass-paneled swing doors. She opened without him having to ring. Perhaps she was listening for the clank of the elevator gate. Like the first time, she led him in silence to the living room, and the two of them sat side by side on the sofa like the other afternoon. The stack of magazines was still there, again with one open in the middle of the sofa.

On the coffee table, two glasses of orange juice. She picked one up and handed it to him. The spot of sunlight was in its place, on the wall behind them. From then on, he would come every day, at the same hour, and each time she'd open the door before he could ring. For years and years. *The Eternal Return of the Same*, a title he'd read on the cover of a philosophy book that his professor, Maurice Caveing, had lent him.

"Is the boy taking his nap?"

And this would be the first thing he'd say to her after taking his seat on the sofa—and this until the end of time.

"No. Tuesday afternoon he's in kindergarten, right near here."

He felt she wanted to add something, but couldn't find the words.

"I was afraid you'd dial the old number, AUTEUIL 15-28, and not the one I gave you."

"No, of course not. I know the difference between day and night."

And it was true that at that hour, in this room, everything seemed clear, simple, and natural.

"The last time, as I was leaving, I thought I walked by Dr. Rouveix in the street. Short, dark hair, tanned skin, with a black bag."

"That's him."

"And was everything all right?"

"Yes. It wasn't really a vaccine, just a booster."

He would have liked the conversation to continue on that same tone all afternoon.

In his hand was his glass of orange juice.

"Shall we toast?"

She gave a brief laugh.

"Gladly."

Their glasses met with a crystalline clink.

He ended up asking:

"Are you planning to stay here for a while?"

"Until the school year starts. I was offered a teaching job in Neuilly, at the Marymount School. Do you know it?"

No, he had never heard of that school. But it didn't matter. Just the name "Marymount" sounded respectable.

"The school is run by Irish nuns. I convinced Mr. Heriford to enroll the boy there. This way, I wouldn't feel like I was abandoning him."

She had spoken the final words in a serious voice, as if she felt responsible for the child.

"I thought a lot about what you said last time. I didn't really answer your questions because I didn't want to meddle in other people's affairs."

She suddenly seemed more mature than her age; and the contrast between her adolescent looks, like a child grown up too fast, and her serious voice called to mind a character in a novel he'd been reading for the past few weeks: *Little Dorrit*.

"Personally, I wonder a lot about those people because I'm responsible for that child."

She swallowed a gulp of orange juice, no doubt to pluck up her courage and tell him what was on her mind.

"I came here through an employment agency special-izing in nannies, governesses, and housekeepers . . . The Stewart Agency . . . "

She knitted her brow, apparently trying to understand a situation that struck her as rather confusing. Wasn't her approach similar to his? Who knew—they might even be able to help each other? She had surely guessed that they were wondering about the same things.

"I don't know very much about Mr. Heriford. At the Stewart Agency, they told me his wife had died or left him."

"And he's never here during the day?"

"Never. I think he goes out very early in the morning. I'm not sure he even sleeps here."

She seemed relieved to be able to confide the de-tails of what she'd observed since starting to care for the child. And every evening, he told himself, when she found herself in the rear bedroom, it must have been stressful to feel she was in terra incognita.

"He merely gave me a number where I could reach him during the day."

He would gladly have asked her to show it to him, but it was probably one of those new, all-digit numbers that leave you in the dark. At least the old-style numbers, with names for prefixes, immediately told you what part of town they were located in. It made research easier.

"Maybe he works in an office."

"Could be."

But she didn't seem very sure.

"You asked about the people who come here after dark. I was able to find out a few names."

She stood up.

"May I? I jotted them down in a notebook."

She went out and he remained alone in the silent, sun-lit room. The window was slightly open and the leaves of the chestnut tree were swaying gently. He stared at the foliage, letting himself be cradled by it. Fifty years later, he still remembered that moment, when time stood still. He also remembered floating in that spring light, when nothing would matter again.

When she came back into the room, he started, as if jerking awake. She again sat next to him. She was holding a school copybook with a sky-blue cover. She opened it and leaned over the lined pages with a studious face.

"Among these names, there is indeed a Mme Hayward. Last time, you told me you knew her."

He was surprised she had remembered the name. It proved that she'd paid careful attention to his every word.

"She comes here often, alone or with her husband, whose name is Philippe Hayward. He's a friend of Mr. Heriford's."

"And is there a Camille Lucas on your list?"

He didn't dare add that her nickname was Death-mask.

"Yes, she's a friend of Mr. Heriford's, too. I can tell you other names."

She consulted her notebook again. Of those names, three meant something to him. Andrée Karvé. Jean Terrail. Guy Vincent. And no doubt a few others, were he to read the list with fresh eyes.

"And, where did you come across all these names?"

"In Mr. Heriford's address book. He left it here last week. Those are surely people who come at night."

She shut the notebook. She was waiting for him to comment, perhaps even give her the solution to a puzzle.

"I'm familiar with some of those names. If you could lend me the list, I'm sure others would ring a bell. And we could have a better sense of what goes on here."

She listened carefully and nodded. He was surprised by so much goodwill.

"It would be better if you didn't come back here at night," she said. "It's too dangerous . . . These people are not very trustworthy."

He felt as if she was worrying about him and trying to protect him. Coming from such a waiflike girl, he found it touching.

"I'll be relieved to start my job at Marymount. And it will be much better for the boy if he's enrolled there."

She was on the verge of confiding something. Finally, she took the plunge:

"I nearly spoke about it with Dr. Rouveix to ask his advice, but now that you're here . . . "

"Honestly, don't worry."

He shrugged and pointed at the half-open window.

"I've never seen such a lovely springtime in Paris."

Her gaze was fixed on the window and the foliage on the chestnut tree. She turned toward him and it seemed that all her anxiety had dissipated.

He wondered whether he had indeed told her at the time: "I've never seen such a lovely springtime in Paris," or whether it was the memory of that spring that led him to write those words today, fifty years later. Chances are, he hadn't said a thing.

"While I'm thinking of it . . . I don't know if this will interest you . . . "

She leafed quickly through the notebook and stopped at a page where apparently she had jotted something down.

"Mr. Heriford is not the tenant of this apartment. A friend of his lent it to him. When I first started working here, two years ago, he sent me out a few times to mail her some letters."

Head bowed over the notebook, she knit her brow, as if trying to read a word that was hard to decipher.

"Her name is Rose-Marie Krawell."

"Ah, I see. And does she live in Paris?"

"The address on the envelopes was somewhere in the South. Does that name mean anything to you?"

"No. Nothing."

He had forced himself to remain poker-faced. After all, she might be laying a trap. But he really had no reason to distrust her, the way he distrusted Deathmask and Martine Hayward.

"And have you ever seen her here?"

"Once, two years ago. She came to see Mr. Heriford. A woman in her fifties, with short blond hair, and she smoked a lot."

He felt like asking if Rose-Marie Krawell still used a lighter, that small, perfumed silver lighter that she'd once lent him, cautioning him to be careful of the flame.

"She spoke very familiarly with Mr. Heriford."

He kept silent, waiting for her to provide further details. But that was all she remembered about Rose-Marie Krawell.

No question, the circle was tightening around him. Had he been alone, he would have felt alarmed; but here, in the company of the person he already thought of as "Little Dorrit," he almost wanted to laugh. So, fifteen years later, Rose-Marie Krawell still owned the house on Rue du Docteur-Kurzenne that Deathmask and Martine Hayward had visited, and also owned this apartment in Auteuil that Deathmask had dragged him to, and on top of that the latter had worked as an accountant in Guy Vincent's office . . . He ended up convincing himself that all those people were weaving a spiderweb in which they hoped to catch him. But for what purpose? And how long had they been on his trail?

"You look worried."

Not really worried. But he felt a certain vertigo at the

sudden appearance of the bonds linking these people to one another, as if on an X-ray screen. In fifteen years, those bonds had branched out, taking on newcomers, and now formed a very tight network that he had unwittingly become part of, as in his childhood.

"We have no reason to worry, neither one of us."

She smiled and took a sip of orange juice.

"By the way, your list wouldn't also contain a certain Michel de Gama, would it? With a *de*?"

She opened the notebook again and reread the first page. After a long pause, she said:

"Not with a *de*."

And she spelled out the name: Michel Degamat.

He now understood why, in the café at Saint-Lazare, the supposed de Gama had reacted so violently when he'd alluded to Vasco de Gama. Michel Degamat. That was no doubt the name that figured on an arrest record, with one photo in frontal view and another in profile and, at the bottom, the date when they were taken at the police precinct. His initial impression might have been correct: this Michel Degamat had known Guy Vincent during a stretch in prison at the time of the house on Rue du Docteur-Kurzenne. If not, where else would they have met? He remembered a telephone conversation he'd overheard one morning while walking by the door to Rose-Marie Krawell's bedroom, especially the phrase: "Guy has just gotten out of prison," a phrase he still heard, fifteen years later, said in the deep and slightly throaty voice of Rose-Marie Krawell. Adults should always speak softly, as you have to watch out for children.

"I'm going to ask you one final question," he said with a smile. "Might you have seen here another friend of Mr. Heriford's, a certain Guy Vincent?"

"Guy Vincent?"

She had spoken the name in a murmur, and that name, coming from so far in the past, produced an odd sensation.

"Very tall, very elegant, hair light brown, or maybe gray."

She knitted her brow again, like a schoolgirl searching for the right answer to a pop quiz.

"A very tall man who looked American?"

"Right."

"Mr. Heriford told me he lived in America. He came here once . . . He brought a present for the boy . . . "

Presents were a habit of Guy Vincent's, from the time of Rue du Docteur-Kurzenne. He remembered the silver-plated compass on which Guy Vincent had had his name engraved: Jean Bosmans. He had kept it for years, until someone stole it from him in one of the boarding schools where he spent his adolescence. He had never gotten over that loss. A compass. Perhaps Guy Vincent thought it would help him find his way through life.

She had shut the notebook again and he decided not

to ask her any more questions, just as he had decided not to explain why he was asking them. He would have been forced to talk about his childhood and the peculiar individuals he'd been around at the time. Someone had written: "We are from our childhood as we are from a country," but you still had to specify what childhood and what country. That would have been difficult for him. And he didn't really have the strength for it, or the desire, that afternoon.

She had glanced at her wristwatch.

"It's almost time for me to go pick up the little one."

"I can accompany you partway . . ."

The two of them took the street where he had encountered Dr. Rouveix a few days earlier. It was the same springlike weather as on that afternoon. He had only to walk with her in the sun and breathe in the light air for those people whose names she had cited to lose any reality. Even if they had led a vague existence in some far-distant past, not a trace of them would remain in the light of the present. And their names would evoke not a single face, for anyone.

She held the notebook in her hand.

"I'm really sorry to have asked you all those questions."

"No, don't be . . . It was a relief to be able to clear the air with you."

She opened her notebook and tore out the first page.

"Here . . . I almost forgot to give you the list of names."

She folded the sheet in four and handed it to him.

"Maybe you'll see other names that will shed even more light. You can tell me next time."

She took his arm as if to guide him.

They had come to Porte d'Auteuil, and she steered him into a street that wasn't familiar, even though he often roamed this neighborhood. They walked along the left-hand sidewalk from which you could make out, behind the buildings, a long stretch of green that must have been a park, or perhaps the start of the Bois de Boulogne. Or simply a prairie. If it hadn't been for the cars parked in front of those buildings, Bosmans might have thought that at the end of this street, they'd find themselves in open country.

She stopped next to a fence on which a copper plaque said: SAINT FRANCIS SCHOOL. KINDERGARTEN. She looked at her watch.

"We should probably part company here. When will you be back?"

"Tomorrow, if you like. At the same time."

She smiled. Behind the fence, she waved to him. He was tempted to wait for them, there, on the sidewalk. He would have liked to get to know the child.

He followed the street in the opposite direction, and it was so calm and rural that he seemed to be walking far from Paris. It was the blue hour, as Guy Vincent would have said.

In the datebook with the green leather cover, the datebook whose year would remain unknown, most of the pages were blank. Guy Vincent had recorded ordinary appointments. Wednesday, January 5: barber. February 18: Eliott Forrest, Hotel Lancaster. March 15: Banville garage. May 14: tailor. Austen, Rue du Colisée. September 18: 9:45, Gaëlle, Gare d'Austerlitz. October 19: 11:00, Jean Terrail, 33 Rue Chardon-Lagache . . . But coming across the page for October 20, his heart leapt. Written there was: Jean Bosmans, 38 Rue du Docteur-Kurzenne. Compass.

That was surely the day when Guy Vincent had given him the compass with his name engraved on the lid. He recalled that it was around the time school started again. He was no longer going to the Jeanne d'Arc school, but to one a bit farther away, the village public school. He kept the compass in the pouch of his smock but avoided showing it to his classmates.

He was surprised to find his name in the datebook amid so many empty pages—and even more so fifteen years after the fact. It was as if a beam of light had finally reached him across all those years, the light of a dead star.

After that October 20, the rest of the pages to the end of the year were blank. He would have loved to have the datebook for the following year, but no doubt there hadn't been one that year. The phrase he'd overheard behind the bedroom door, which Rose-Marie Krawell had said into the telephone in her throaty voice: "Guy has just gotten out of prison," was from long after he'd been given the compass.

It was a summer afternoon. He remembered the spot of sunlight on the bedroom door, and slowly crawling across it a fly, from which he couldn't detach his gaze. He didn't dare move. A day of heat and holiday. July or August, for certain. A summer that, with distance, had become timeless. What use was it trying to recall the exact month or year? He remained there, frozen, facing the spot of sunlight on the door.

Toward the end of the 1990s, Bosmans had received the following letter:

Dear Sir:

I am a reader of yours, and I have noticed that on more than one occasion you have mentioned a certain Guy Vincent, whom you sometimes call Roger Vincent. I believe it is the same person.

I imagine there must be several Guy (or Roger) Vincents in France, but from what you have written about your "character," I am convinced that the Guy Vincent (or Roger) in your books is indeed the one I knew long ago. This is why I have taken the liberty of writing to you.

I met Guy Vincent at the Lycée Pasteur in Neuilly. We were both sixteen and in sophomore year. He was a likable boy, a tad reckless, something of a "troublemaker," as they say, but always quick to lend a hand or help people out when they were short of cash. He had left school midyear to enroll in a private course, where I occasionally went to pick him up. He'd take me to the Balzac Cinema to see American films, and to various cafés on the Champs-Elysées or in Montparnasse, where he was already a regular at seventeen. One time I accompanied him home, to an apartment near Place Pereire, where he lived with his mother. He told me she was of American origin. Guy was on the junior (?) or varsity (?) ski team, and he once sent me a picture of himself at a competition, which I'm enclosing.

And then the war started and we lost track of each other. I ran into him by chance sometime after the Liberation. He told me he was working at the American Embassy. He was married by then, and I got together several times with him and his wife, Gaëlle. They lived in a small private hotel near Boulevard Berthier. Guy told me the American Embassy had requisitioned it for him. After that, I figured he'd left France, as his home telephone no longer answered. The American Embassy, where I tried to reach him, had never heard of him. I've had no further word of him since, nor of his wife.

Except around ten years later, through a prosecutor friend of mine who'd been in our class at Pasteur. He told me Guy had had legal troubles, more than once, notably for being mixed up in a huge scam "involving money orders," but when my friend tried to explain the details I didn't understand any of it. On

top of which, if I knew Guy, he wouldn't have under-
stood it either. That's why I believe in his innocence.

I don't know if he's still alive. Neither of us is
very young anymore, as you can imagine. Maybe
he's gotten in touch with you because of your books.
In any case, I can attest that he was what they call
a fine boy.

The letter, signed with the initials N. F., was accompanied by the photo of a very young man in a ski outfit. On
the back of the photo was written in black ink: Megève,
February 1940. University ski championship. Roche-
brune descent. Vincent 2nd place, behind Rigaud and
Dalmas de Polignac ex aequo.

One evening, Camille asked him some insidious questions. She had left her job at Saint-Lazare, as well as her address. She now had a room at 65 Quai de la Tournelle, a squat old building that served as a hotel, where she appeared to be the sole guest. Her window looked out on the Seine. She had ultimately found work as an accountant in a large garage on Fossés-Saint-Bernard.

She hadn't given any clear explanation for this sudden retreat to the Left Bank, other than she felt like "a change of scenery." When he'd asked her in a sarcastic tone whether it wasn't to "burn her bridges" with Michel de Gama and the Hotel Chatham, she had merely nodded, with no further comment.

That evening, in a tiny Vietnamese restaurant on Rue des Grands-Degrés, near the quay, the conversation veered toward a subject about which he felt he'd best exercise some caution.

They had just sat at their table when she said flat out:

"There's something I want to know: why did you steal that datebook and photo from that fellow Guy Vincent?"

He immediately realized that she'd wanted to ask it for a long time and had finally taken the plunge. Up until then, he'd thought she simply didn't care.

"I've started work on a novel and I need specific objects for inspiration. That photo and datebook help spark my imagination."

He had endeavored to sound as serious and convincing as possible.

"But why Guy Vincent?"

She persisted in a way that he found suspicious. He'd have to weigh his words carefully.

"The photo and datebook make it easier for me to create a fictional character. It could have been anyone. Like that guy Michel de Gama, for instance. Or you."

"Really?"

She was looking at him strangely. She didn't seem the least bit convinced. He guessed she was dying to ask something else, something that could put him in a tight spot.

"I leafed through Guy Vincent's datebook. Why was your name on one of the pages?"

"Yes, funny, isn't it . . . But Bosmans is a very common name in Belgium and northern France."

She seemed disconcerted. He had answered in a calm voice. He added:

"And besides, that datebook must be a good twenty years old . . . Back then, I was probably still in the cradle . . ."

She smiled slightly.

"Yes, but it was the same first name."

"Everybody's named Jean."

There was a long silence, which would have seemed heavier to him had the radio not been playing on the restaurant counter, as usual.

"And what's even weirder is the address he wrote down—the same address as the house we visited the other day with Martine Hayward."

"Oh, really? Are you sure?"

He'd done his best to look astonished, but he was tired of playing this game.

"I'm absolutely sure."

Again she was looking at him strangely.

"Maybe he went to that house too."

But he sensed that he'd said too much.

"Maybe."

She shrugged. And the conversation took a more normal turn. She told him about her accounting job in the garage on Rue des Fossés-Saint-Bernard and admitted how happy she was to be living in this neighborhood from now on.

On another evening, they were walking along Quai de la Tournelle and Quai de Montebello. A spring evening. And he remarked that, all in all, you could feel the softness of that season by walking along the river and the little adjacent streets better than you could at Saint-Lazare and Pigalle.

She suddenly asked him:

"Are you happy, Jean?"

"Yes."

At that moment, he had an urge to answer the questions she'd asked in the Vietnamese restaurant with full honesty. Yes, the Jean Bosmans whose name figured in Guy Vincent's datebook was indeed he. And at the time, I lived in the house you and Martine Hayward visited, at 38 Rue du Docteur-Kurzenne.

He distrusted Camille, even though she wished him no ill. She withheld certain things from him, but it gave her a peculiar charm. One of his bedside books, along with Cardinal de Retz's *Memoirs* and a few others, was a treatise on morals called *The Art of Not Speaking*. Ever since childhood, he had always tried to practice that particular art, a very difficult art, the one he admired most and that could be applied to any domain, even literature. Hadn't his professor taught him that prose and poetry are made not only of words, but especially of silences?

From their very first meeting, he had noticed that Camille had a great aptitude for silence. Normally, people say way too much. He had quickly understood that she would never say anything about her past, her relationships, how she spent her time, and maybe even her work as an accountant. He didn't resent her for it. One likes people just as they are. Even if they inspire a certain distrust. Still, one detail bothered him: the moment when he'd found himself with Camille in Guy Vincent's office at the Hotel Chatham. He'd been reminded of those life-sized figures on display at the Grévin Wax Museum: he, sitting at the desk on which stood a photo of Guy Vincent in a leather frame, one of its drawers about to reveal the datebooks and sheets of letterhead with his name on them. At the Grévin Museum, they would have called the tableau: "A Visitor to Guy Vincent's Office." And he wondered whether Michel de Gama and Camille hadn't concocted the scene beforehand, using old accessories, perfectly aware that once, in his childhood, he'd known Guy Vincent. And besides, his name, Jean Bosmans, with the address of the house on Rue du Docteur-Kurzenne, figured on a page of the datebook, and they knew it. But why would they have taken all the trouble to reconstruct

"Guy Vincent's office" in his honor? Camille must have had some idea.

That spring evening, after following the quays, they had taken Rue Saint-Julien-le-Pauvre. And he decided to ask her, without much hope of getting an answer:

"Don't you think it was strange, our visit to that Guy Vincent fellow's old office?"

She had taken his arm and he felt her fingers clench.

"It felt like a scene from the Grévin Museum."

He'd hoped that remark would make her relax, even encourage her to open up to him. But no, nothing. She remained mute.

They had arrived next to the garden adjoining the Greek church. She looked up at him.

"Jean . . . you need to be careful. There are people who are out to harm you."

She had said it very fast, and not in the calm, drawling voice she normally used. He hadn't expected that.

"And who are these people? Michel Degamat, perhaps? 'Degamat' all one word?"

He had said it looking her straight in the eye, but she again kept silent. They turned back toward the quays. As they walked, she squeezed his arm more tightly. Clearly she practiced the art of not speaking almost as well as he did. Still, they could understand each other without spelling things out.

Deathmask—or rather Camille, for ultimately he got tired of writing her nickname—left Paris for a few days. She told him her boss was sending her to Bordeaux to check the books at another of his garages. At first, he didn't think to ask whether she was lying to explain her absence. It was only the next day, after she'd left, that he started wondering.

At around noon, there was a knock at the door of the room on Quai de la Tournelle, and when he opened it, he was surprised to see Martine Hayward standing there.

"Hello, Jean."

She had never called him by his first name, and since Camille had started living in this room he'd never seen the two of them together in the neighborhood.

He asked her in, and she sat on the edge of the bed, as if the room was familiar to her.

"Forgive me for dropping by unannounced, but I have a favor to ask."

She gave him a sheepish smile.

"I know Camille is away, otherwise I would have asked her."

He remained standing in front of her, perplexed at seeing her sitting on that bed, in that room. He suddenly had the feeling that it was her room and that he was the outsider.

"I'm moving into the house we went to see two weeks ago. Do you remember, Jean? And I happen to have lost my driver's license along with some other papers."

It was as if she were reciting a text she'd just learned and was unsure of the words.

"I still have a few things to pick up at my husband's hotel, near Chevreuse, where we stopped off last time. And then drop them at my new house. Would you mind driving me?"

He didn't know what to say. Her insistence on calling him "Jean" struck him as suspicious.

"My car is downstairs. I drove it here from Auteuil without a license, afraid I'd get pulled over."

"Auteuil?"

"Yes, of course, Jean. During the move, I've been spending the night at the apartment in Auteuil."

No doubt about it, the same places kept recurring. He briefly thought of Kim and the sunlit afternoons. And since Martine Hayward was seated on the bed, he was tempted to ask her what happened at night at the apartment in Auteuil.

"You understand, Jean . . . it's a long way to go without

a license, all the way to the Vallée de Chevreuse. It would be wiser for you to drive. I know I'm being silly, but I've always had a fear of being pulled over by the police."

The same route, in the same car. But he wasn't in the same frame of mind as the first time, and he felt a certain apprehension at the prospect of seeing the house on Rue du Docteur-Kurzenne again. He remembered the moment he'd gone into "Guy Vincent's office" with Camille, sitting there like a wax figure in the Grévin Museum. And now it was Martine Hayward who was dragging him to the scene of his past, Martine Hayward whom he mistrusted much more than he did Camille, and whose hidden agenda was much harder to guess.

This time, they left Paris via Porte de Châtillon. He knew the way, but he hadn't driven in a long time. He wondered whether he even had his license in his wallet, and he decided not to check. In any case, he was covered by a kind of immunity, as in dreams where, if things go bad, you can always wake up.

They entered the Vallée de Chevreuse. He could feel it in the freshness of the air and the soft light, green and gold, filtering through the leaves of the trees. Yes, it was perhaps the feeling of returning to the past after fifteen years.

"Do you spend a lot of time at that apartment in Auteuil?"

Under the calming influence of the Vallée de Chevreuse, through which he felt as if he were gliding not in a car but rather along a river, in a canoe, he no longer really distrusted Martine Hayward.

"You know, I'm sort of René-Marco's secretary and business partner . . . His apartment is pretty large . . . It's a meeting place . . . a kind of club where people get together at night."

"A house of assignation?"

"Yes. Let's call it a house of assignation."

She shrugged, and he understood that she didn't feel like saying any more. But after a long pause:

"René-Marco is a friend of my husband's. He has a little boy, but his wife left him two years ago. How shall I put this? He's not very stable and he lives on the edge. Kind of like my husband . . . "

He was surprised to hear such an admission from her. Then, as if she wanted to make him forget what she'd just said:

"But here's something strange . . . The owner of the house I've rented is the same as for the Auteuil apartment."

She had turned toward him and was smiling. Perhaps she was watching for a reaction.

"Anyway, I guess it makes sense, since she's René-Marco's godmother."

"Do you know her?"

He had asked the question in an indifferent tone of voice.

"Not really. I must have seen her once at René-Marco's. Someone named Rose-Marie Krawell."

Her eyes rested on him, without his being able to tell whether she was trying to gauge what effect the name would have on him.

"René-Marco borrowed a lot of money from her. And my husband, too. They were all close when they were younger."

She seemed to be talking to herself. Or was she trying to win his trust so that he'd start talking as well?

"Now she lives on the Riviera."

"Do you have her address?"

"No, why?"

He regretted asking that question. But he hadn't been able to resist.

"Because her name sounds vaguely familiar."

Again, her eyes fixed on him. Perhaps she was waiting for him to be more specific. Or maybe she was just looking at him, with no ulterior motive. Unable to decide, he kept silent for the rest of the trip.

He parked the car right by the steps of the Moulin-de-Vert-Cœur Inn, and from up close the building seemed even more dilapidated than it had the first time. He followed her into the entrance foyer. At the other end was the reception. Room keys hung from the wall. She took one down in passing and they climbed a wide stairway whose bannisters and steps were made of light-colored wood. The hotel entrance looked as if the guests had fled on the eve of a declaration of war or a revolution.

On the second floor, she opened the door to Room 16. Foliage from a tree was poking through a partly open window. The guests would not be coming back; the hotel was surrounded by a forest, whose vegetation would gradually invade the restaurant, the reception area, the stairway, and the rooms. A closet stood wide open, its shelves bare. In a corner of the room, next to the window, a sofa with a fur coverlet. A desk facing the window, and behind the desk, an armchair on which sat a black leather suitcase, the same size as the one Martine Hayward had come to get the first time.

"As you see, I don't have much luggage."

She had sat on the edge of the sofa. She motioned for him to come sit beside her.

"This is the last time I'll be in this room."

There was a gust of wind and one of the window panels banged against the wall. She had moved closer to him and rested her head on his shoulder. She whispered in his ear:

"If you only knew how sad my life has been . . . "

Then she pulled him down on the sofa, a low, wide sofa like the ones in the Auteuil apartment.

*　　*　　*

As they entered the village, after passing by the town hall and over the railroad crossing, he felt vaguely apprehensive. Perhaps she had laid a trap for him, and in the house on Rue du Docteur-Kurzenne, Michel de Gama and his stooges were waiting for him, having prepared, as at the Hotel Chatham, another tableau worthy of the Grévin Museum: "Returning after Fifteen Years to the House of His Childhood." And he'd finally understand what these people wanted from him.

But when he arrived at the top of the sloping alley and parked the car, he felt certain there was no danger. The street was silent and deserted.

He got out of the car with her and grabbed the black leather suitcase from the back seat. He crossed behind her through the small gate leading from the street, climbed the three steps, and set the luggage down on the porch.

"I'll wait for you in the car."

At first she looked surprised that he didn't want to come in, then she smiled at him.

And before she'd even opened the door, he turned back toward the street.

And now, the same route to get back to Paris: Les Metz, the hangars and runway of the Villacoublay aerodrome, behind which he could make out the Cour Roland, the Homme Mort woods, then the lawns and vegetable gardens of Montcel, the Val d'Enfer, and the Bièvre flowing with the burble of a waterfall. And, farther still, the Vallée de Chevreuse.

She looked straight ahead at the road.

"I understand why you didn't want to come inside the house. It brought back too many memories."

He might have been surprised by those words, the first she'd spoken since they'd left Rue du Docteur-Kurzenne. So she knew everything, and suddenly he found that perfectly natural and expected, as in dreams when you already know what people are going to tell you, since everything is starting over again and they've already said it in another life.

"No need to say anything, Jean. I understand."

Yes, no need to say anything. They had reached Petit-Clamart, where he had once taken a bus to Paris after walking for miles, the day he ran away from boarding school.

"I didn't want to make you feel bad earlier . . . But Rose-Marie Krawell died last year."

Feel bad? He didn't really, even though he had memories of the woman in the house on Rue du Docteur-Kurzenne. He had hoped Kim would give him her address on the Riviera, since she had mailed letters from "René-Marco" there. Maybe she even knew her telephone number. He'd once dreamed he called her. Her voice sounded far away, like the voices on the "network" at AUTEUIL 15-28, but she answered most of his questions. On-and-off silence and static, and each time he thought the connection had been dropped; but then Rose-Marie Krawell's voice came back much clearer, before fading out again. What had become of Guy Vincent? "He went back to America for good, darling." She called him "darling" or "my boy." She said: "And you, my boy, what have you been up to?" And just as he was about to answer, the line went dead.

Night was falling when they arrived at Porte de Châtillon. He asked where he should take her.

"To the Auteuil apartment."

She let out a sigh. The prospect didn't seem to appeal to her. She had said "the Auteuil apartment" the way she might have said "the office."

"But next week, I'm definitely moving into the house."

She turned and looked at him sadly.

"I don't suppose you'll ever come see me there."

It was the first time she'd addressed him with the familiar *tu*. He didn't answer.

"I'll let you know if I find anything in the house that might interest you."

Again he didn't answer. That sentence, which she had said in a natural tone, a tone of ordinary conversation, suddenly made him feel anxious.

He walked her to the door of the building, but then she took his arm.

"Can we walk a little?"

They went up the street, as he'd done the other afternoon when he had crossed paths with Dr. Rouveix.

"Camille tells me you went to the Hotel Chatham one evening, to Guy Vincent's office."

She had said "Guy Vincent's office" in a sarcastic tone and she gave out a brief laugh.

"You know, Guy Vincent never had an office."

She fell silent. She seemed worried. He thought she was struggling to find her words and was about to tell him some bad news: "I didn't want to make you feel bad, but Guy Vincent is dead." And it's true that it would have made him feel bad. A final link would be broken and a period of his past would have been definitively swallowed up, while he remained on the shore, alone and orphaned. But orphaned from what? He wouldn't have been able to say exactly.

"Guy Vincent disappeared a long time ago . . . He went back to America . . . He must be living there under another name."

He felt like thanking her for such good news. And besides, she confirmed what he had known all along.

They were now heading down the street in the opposite direction, like people who don't want to part company and keep walking each other home back and forth. It could go on forever.

"Apparently you witnessed something, fifteen years ago, in that house on Rue du Docteur-Kurzenne."

She halted and looked him in the eye.

"Those morons . . . I'm talking about Michel de Gama, René-Marco, and even my husband . . . have been trying to get in touch with you."

She took his arm again, squeezing it tighter. And, in a lower voice:

"They asked us, me and Camille, to act as go-betweens."

He still didn't quite understand, but he really hoped she was going to clarify things.

"Those three morons knew Guy Vincent when they were very young . . . in Poissy Prison."

She seemed reluctant to continue, as if ashamed of providing these details. He would have liked to reassure her: with him, Bosmans, there was no need for such scruples.

"When they got out of prison, Guy Vincent helped

them out. My husband and de Gama more or less served as his drivers or errand boys. That was around the time you lived in that house. They want to know if you saw anything that happened there."

Right, he had understood. There was no further need for her to clarify. They had arrived in front of the building.

"They only want to ask you some questions. They're just a bunch of idiotic amateurs. They think you're going to tell them where the treasure is buried."

She leaned her face close to his.

"I hope they don't hurt you. In any case, watch your back."

She brushed his cheek with her lips and gently ran her hand over his brow. Before the entrance door closed on her, she gave him a wave of farewell.

He headed toward the Porte d'Auteuil metro stop. He waited for the red light before crossing the boulevard and found himself in front of the picture window of Murat's. It was 11 p.m. and there were few remaining diners in the restaurant. At a table on the glassed-in terrace, just behind the window, he noticed three men. He immediately recognized Michel de Gama and René-Marco Heriford. The third man he saw only in profile.

Then, feeling dizzy, he walked into the restaurant and planted himself next to their table.

Michel de Gama jumped slightly, but then smiled: "Well, well, to what do we owe the pleasure?"

He indicated the other two.

"I believe you know René-Marco. And this is Philippe Hayward, Martine's husband. How funny, we were just talking about you. I was telling my friends that you're awfully elusive."

The three men stared at him in silence.

"Did you leave Camille back in the apartment?" Michel de Gama asked sarcastically. "Here, have a seat."

But he remained standing by their table. He could no longer move, as if in a bad dream. René-Marco and Philippe Hayward didn't take their eyes off him.

"Have a seat. We've wanted to ask you something for a very long time. And I hope you'll answer. You are surely a boy with a very good memory and I'm counting on you to enlighten us."

Michel de Gama had said this in a brusque tone, as if giving him orders or threats. And all of a sudden, he felt his paralysis lift and he regained some of his agility.

"Hold on . . . I'll be right back . . . "

And with supple steps, he headed for the restaurant door. On the threshold, he turned back. The three others were staring at him, wide-eyed. He was tempted to give them the finger.

Just as he was crossing the boulevard, he saw Michel de Gama running after him. He wondered whether he was armed. He started running as well and dove into the metro station. He hurtled down the steps and was lucky enough to catch a waiting train.

*   *   *

Back in his room on Quai de la Tournelle, he felt relieved to be on the other bank of the Seine. He stretched out on the bed. What could Camille be doing at that moment, in Bordeaux or wherever she was? A tour boat passed by, its beam of light projecting lattice-shaped reflections on the wall, reflections he had often seen in his childhood, gliding over a similar wall at the passage of the same tour boat. But another memory from that time emerged into the light, like strange flowers floating to the surface of stagnant waters.

He again heard Martine Hayward say in her slightly husky voice: "Apparently you witnessed something, fifteen years ago." It was his last day in the house on Rue du Docteur-Kurzenne. From a window on the second floor that looked out on the small courtyard, he saw two men leaning over a well, one of them holding a flashlight. They were joined by another, who had just inspected the terraced gardens. They had searched every room in the house, even his childhood bedroom. A uniformed officer was at the wheel of a black sedan parked in front of the house, but the others were wearing street clothes. Except for them, there was no one in the house: not Rose-Marie Krawell, not Guy Vincent, not those whose names he'd remembered much later and whom he'd often seen there. Annie, Jeannette Coudreuse, Jean Sergent, Suzanne Bouquereau, Denise Bartholomeus, Mme Karvé, Eliott Forrest . . . When he thought of that day after all these years, he was still amazed the police hadn't questioned him.

He was standing in the hallway and he had surprised one of them, who was coming down from the third floor and had surely searched the room with the skylight, where Annie often slept. The man had patted his shoulder and said, "What are you doing here, kid?" Then he went to join the others. It hadn't occurred to that one, either, to question him. In any case, Bosmans wouldn't have answered. No doubt it was on that day that he started practicing, without yet realizing it, the art of not speaking.

They had done masonry work, toward the end of that winter, on the right-hand wall of the bedroom with the skylight. One afternoon, through the half-open door, he had spied them boring a large hole in the wall. But he hadn't dared enter. From his room, for several days running, he had heard hammer blows and the sound of falling rubble. One night, when everyone was asleep, he had slipped into the hallway and crept upstairs. The room with the skylight was locked. A few days later, after lunch, he had surreptitiously gone into the room. The wall was smooth and white as it had always been. No trace of the large hole that they'd bored in the wall, behind which he imagined a secret chamber.

Guy Vincent lived in the house during that entire time. He occupied Rose-Marie Krawell's large bedroom on the second floor. People came to see him; they parked their cars on Rue du Docteur-Kurzenne but left without spending the night. Bosmans didn't recall any of their faces. Besides, he was at school most of the time. It was apparently Guy Vincent who oversaw the construction in the room with the skylight. He had heard his voice several times when he went into the hall, but he had never dared go upstairs, even though he knew Guy Vincent would not yell at him.

And then, one Saturday when he didn't go to school, he had seen, from his bedroom window, a covered van stop in front of the house. Two men got out and started unloading crates and big canvas sacks. Through the door of his room, he could hear them coming upstairs slowly, with the crates and sacks, up to the bedroom with the skylight. They had to make several trips. Over the following days, the construction work went on nonstop.

He was still lying on the bed and had switched off the bedside lamp. Camille had left on the nightstand the small pink pillbox she occasionally opened to take out a pill, which she swallowed while tossing back her head. He hoped that in Bordeaux or wherever she was she wouldn't be suffering withdrawal. And then he repeated to himself what Martine Hayward had said: "They're just a bunch of idiotic amateurs. They think you're going to tell them where the treasure is buried." He almost pitied them. Once more the lattice-like reflections slid over the wall. The tour boat was back. He remembered another wall, smooth and white, in the room with the skylight. "What are you doing here, kid?" the cop had said. And he, he knew exactly where they had made the huge hole and plastered it up, but in those days, no one thought to listen to what children had to say.

In Nice, one December. But he was unsure of the year. 1980? 1981? He remembered that it had been raining constantly for ten days. He had taken a taxi to go to the city center. Coming upon Square Alsace-Lorraine, the driver, who had been silent until then, abruptly said:

"I always feel blue when I come past here."

His voice was husky, and his accent Parisian. A dark-haired man in his forties. Bosmans had been surprised by the confession. The man had stopped the cab at the edge of the square.

"You see that building, there on the left?"

He pointed to a building, one of whose façades faced the square and another Boulevard Victor-Hugo.

"For two years, I was a lady's chauffeur. She died there in a little apartment on the fourth floor."

Bosmans didn't know what to say to that. Finally:

"Had the lady lived in Nice a long time?"

The taxi continued up Boulevard Victor-Hugo. The man drove slowly.

"Oh, you know, sir . . . It's complicated. She'd lived in Paris when she was young . . . Then she came to the Riviera . . . First to Cannes, in a big villa in La Californie . . . Then a hotel . . . And then Square Alsace-Lorraine, in that tiny apartment."

"Was she French?"

"Yes. On both sides, even though she had a foreign name."

"A foreign name?"

"Yes. Her name was Rose-Marie Krawell."

Bosmans thought to himself that a dozen years earlier, that name would have startled him. But since then, in the rare moments when certain details of his previous lives came to mind, it was as if he now saw them only through frosted glass.

"Toward the end, I would wait for her in the car, in front of the house. She didn't want to leave her apartment."

"Why not?"

"Beauties like that can't stand getting old."

"Do you think it's only beautiful women who can't stand getting old?"

Saying that, Bosmans had forced a laugh, but it was a nervous one.

"She didn't want to see anyone anymore. If I hadn't been there, she would have let herself starve to death."

"And what about Mr. Krawell?"

The driver turned toward Bosmans, no doubt surprised that he'd remembered the name.

"Her husband was long dead. She inherited big from him."

"And do you know what this Mr. Krawell did in life?"

"A huge fur concern, something like that. But that was a long time ago. Before and during the war."

As a child, Bosmans had never heard this man spoken of. And besides, why would he have wondered at that age whether there was a Mr. Krawell?

"The saddest part is, toward the end of her life, she was mixing in bad company."

He had already heard that expression from someone.

"Bad company?"

"Yes, sir. People who only wanted her money. It happens here a lot, with former beauties."

"Former beauties?"

"Yes, sir."

So Rose-Marie Krawell was a former beauty. That qualifier wouldn't have occurred to Bosmans at the time of Rue du Docteur-Kurzenne.

"You said you're going to the center. Shall I drop you at the Hotel des Postes? Would that do?"

"That's fine," Bosmans answered mechanically.

The driver stopped in front of the Hotel des Postes and turned around toward Bosmans again.

"Can I show you a picture?"

He took it out of his wallet and handed it to Bosmans.

"It's a photo of Mme Krawell when she was very young, with her husband and a friend, at Eze-sur-Mer. Mme Krawell gave it to me."

The three figures were seated at a table on the terrace of a beachside restaurant. Bosmans didn't recognize Rose-Marie Krawell. Very young, indeed. Only her eyes were the same as when she would look at him, in another life. He immediately recognized Guy Vincent. The third person, older, face long and thin, hair slicked back, fine mustache, must have been Mr. Krawell. The driver took the photo, delicately, between his thumb and forefinger, and carefully slid it back into his wallet.

"Forgive me for bothering you with all this . . . But every time I go by Square Alsace-Lorraine . . . "

Leaving the taxi, Bosmans felt so unsettled that he didn't know which way to walk. Much later, after many detours, he found himself in Place Garibaldi, without having noticed the long path he'd followed. He had walked for almost an hour in the rain.

The words "Hold on . . . I'll be right back": he would often say them after that incident, without ever keeping his promise, and each time they would mark a break in his life. On the nights he spent alone on Quai de la Tournelle, the image of those individuals at the table behind the restaurant window, and that of Michel de Gama pursuing him as he dove into the metro station—those images surged two or three times in his dreams. There would be similar ruptures and flights over the following years, and they could be summarized in two sentences that he repeated to himself: "This joke has gone on long enough," and especially: "Time to burn my bridges." And for many years, his life followed that staccato rhythm.

There was no further word from Camille. It seemed to Bosmans that she had left behind, in the room, a smell of ether, that odor at once fresh and heavy that he had known since childhood. Summer had begun. On July 1, he got up at around seven. He packed a travel bag with the few clothes that were his. And, from Quai de la Tournelle, he walked to the Gare de Lyon on one of those radiant mornings that can make you forget everything.

At the station, he bought a second-class ticket for Saint-Raphaël. The train departed at 9:15. It was the first day of summer break and there were no empty seats in the compartments. He remained standing in the corridor, and when he saw pass below him the buildings of narrow Rue Coriolis, he felt as if he was leaving something of himself behind and quitting Paris forever.

From Saint-Raphaël, a bus that skirted the edge of the sea, then followed roads with sharp bends that seemed like mountain paths, left him in a village in the Massif des Maures. Night had fallen and he found a room to rent on the main square, above the café. Soon the lights in the café went out and all was silent. No one would come looking for him here, not Michel de Gama, not René-Marco Heriford, not Philippe Hayward, all of whom he thought could be dangerous, like most morons.

Before falling asleep, he tried to recap the various events of the previous months. The apartment in Auteuil, the Vallée de Chevreuse, and Rue du Docteur-Kurzenne suddenly seemed like distant lands to him. He started laughing hysterically at the thought that any day now, those three "morons" would go to the house Martine Hayward had rented and try to find the secret hiding place where Guy Vincent had stashed his treasure. If the police had failed fifteen years earlier, those half-wits would hardly fare better, short of demolishing every wall in the house with a steam drill. They must have thought they were playing "their last card," but when it came to "cards," you had only to look at them to tell that they'd never turned up a good hand in their lives.

He woke up very early the next morning. The café wasn't yet open on the small, empty square. He walked through the sleeping village and passed by the post office. He suddenly felt like sending them a telegram, addressed to the Hotel Chatham or the apartment in Auteuil:

GOOD LUCK. BE SURE TO LET ME KNOW WHEN YOU'VE FOUND IT.

But the post office was open only from three to five in the afternoon, and they would know where the telegram had been sent from. They would come here to get him and drag him back to Paris by force.

A few tables had been set out in front of the café, and he sat at one of them. After these past uncertain months, he told himself he'd stay a long time in this village, and that from time to time he'd take the bus to go swimming on the beaches of the gulf.

He had packed a pad of letter paper in his travel bag. Early one very hot afternoon, he was sitting at a table of the café, on the little square, in the shade, and he wrote the first sentence of what might become a novel. Then he jotted down a few random notes. He wanted to give an account of what he'd recently experienced. Previously forgotten childhood memories come back to you after fifteen years, and you become an amnesiac who has regained a scrap of memory. You owe this to certain persons whose existence you'd known nothing about and who are looking for you, because *they* know that fifteen years earlier you witnessed something. Fifteen years is a long time, long enough for other witnesses to have disappeared. But these persons who need your testimony have not gone in search of lost time for the same reasons as you. Between those "morons" and you, there is a failure to communicate. And you can't really understand them or act as their guide, even though each of you has started down the same road toward the past.

Very early one morning, he boarded the first bus that headed down to the gulf and got off at La Foux. Then he walked along the shore road and soon ended up on the beach at Pampelonne.

In that distant early July, the beach at that hour was still deserted. He swam and lay down on the sand, near a row of bamboo cabanas and some tables, each one shaded by a parasol. From a larger cabana that served as bar, a man emerged and walked toward him, a man in his fifties, dressed in a Hawaiian shirt and red shorts.

The man walked by, staring at him, and Bosmans thought he would keep going. But after a moment, he retraced his steps.

"How is it?"

"Very nice."

"Ideal time for a swim."

He knitted his brow.

"Don't I know you . . . ? I think we used to get together, with Camille Lucas . . . "

And Bosmans recognized him as well. A man that Camille had introduced as "Dr. Robbes," with whom they'd had lunch a couple of times at Wepler. He had invited them to his home, on a small street that led into the Bois de Boulogne. Bosmans hesitated for a moment. He wanted to cut the conversation short and tell the man, "No, sir, you must be mistaken," but he felt bad about lying to him. The times they'd met, he'd seemed to exert a good influence on Camille. A very courteous gentleman, with the austere suits and reassuring face of a notary or provincial pharmacist, or even a university professor. He had never quite understood under what circumstances Camille had met him, but it was surely not in the entourage of Michel de Gama, René-Marco Heriford, or Philippe Hayward.

"Dr. Robbes?"

"Yes, of course."

To be sure, his Hawaiian shirt and red shorts were quite a change from the strict outfits he wore in Paris.

Bosmans stood up and shook his hand.

"And Camille?"

"She's in Paris, but she'll be coming to join me soon."

Why had he said that?

"I'd be delighted to see her. Come have lunch with us whenever you like. Any day at all, at around one. With Camille or by yourself. Over there, you see it?"

He pointed to the row of bamboo cabanas and the tables.

They shook hands and he headed back toward the cabanas. After a few yards, he turned around:

"It's nice here, isn't it? You know that line of Rimbaud:
'Come, the wines are flowing to the shore' . . . ?"

And he waved.

"Come have lunch with us." Bosmans wondered what he
had meant by "us." His friends? And he regretted that
Camille wasn't there on that beach, with the prospect
of the two of them lunching "any day at all, at around
one" in the company of Dr. Robbes. And of talking about
Rimbaud.

He didn't really know exactly what the relationship
was between Camille and Dr. Robbes. She had confided
to him that Dr. Robbes "did favors for a lot of people." He
wrote prescriptions for her for a medication intended
to counteract the adverse effects of the pills in the little
pink boxes—at least that's what he had understood. And
Camille called the mix of that medication and those pills
a "cocktail."

Where had she met Dr. Robbes? In the pharmaceuti-
cal laboratory he headed, when she was doing some accounting work there, she said.

He left the beach in early afternoon, just as the holi-
day-makers were starting to show up en masse. He followed the same path in the opposite direction to La
Foux, where he waited for the bus that would take him
back to the village.

No, it wasn't very prudent to go swimming at Pampelonne and see Dr. Robbes again. Or Camille, for that matter. He didn't trust her enough to propose she join him here. She might alert the others. But other calm, secret beaches existed in the gulf, where, safe from everything, you could let yourself glide into the heart of summer.

In the mornings, in the village, he worked on his book, in his room or outdoors at one of the café tables. The book had a provisional title: *The Dark of Summer*. And in fact, there was a contrast between the light of the Midi and that of the Paris streets where the shady characters he'd known went about their business. As the pages accumulated, he slid these characters into a parallel world where he had nothing to fear from them. He'd been no more than a nocturnal spectator who ended up writing down everything he'd seen, guessed, or imagined around him.

He wondered whether he should have begun writing his book in Paris, in the room on Quai de la Tournelle. It would have been difficult under the constant threat of the three "morons," whose last image haunted him: the three of them, together behind the restaurant window, at night, and one of them chasing him all the way to the metro.

He would gladly have stayed in the South until the end of summer, writing on white pages in the blue ink of his pen. This sun and this light allowed him to see more clearly and not get lost, as he did in Paris. But he was out of money.

He was tempted to go back to the beach at Pampelonne and find Dr. Robbes. He'd explain his situation, and maybe the man would help him prolong his stay. He quickly gave up on the idea. He had to manage without anyone's help, and solitude was the necessary condition for finishing his book. He was afraid Dr. Robbes would talk about Camille and suggest she come join them, which he wanted to avoid, knowing full well that Camille's presence threatened to drag him back to his former life.

He caught a train for Paris after August 15. The train left very early and, unlike the trip down, the compartments were half empty. That evening at the Gare de Lyon, the moment he set foot on the platform, he felt as if he were arriving in the city for the first time, even though he knew it down to the last street. He had almost finished writing his book, and in this book he had rid himself of all the weight and blackness of the previous years.

He had only twenty centimes left, not enough for a metro ticket, but it contributed to his feeling of lightness. He crossed the Seine and reached the southern neighborhoods via Avenue d'Italie. Now and then he sat on a bench and watched the passersby surrounding him, the building façades, and the few cars circulating.

He walked to Rue de la Voie-Verte, after Parc Montsouris and La Tombe-Issoire, and there he went into a small hotel where he'd once stayed. He rediscovered the ancient elevator, and the room looked a lot like the one he'd had in the village in the Maures. When he opened the window and the green shutters because of the heat, the August evening was the same in Paris as over there.

The next morning he got up early. The evening before, while hanging his clothes in the room's narrow closet, he had come across a five-franc bill at the bottom of a trouser pocket. He took the metro, getting off at Franklin-Roosevelt station.

Since the previous year, he'd been wearing a wristwatch of some value that he'd found in the drawer of a nightstand in a room of the Hotel Roma on Rue Caulaincourt. It was the winter when he'd met Camille Lucas, aka Deathmask. Was it her influence? He had not brought the watch to the reception desk, but had kept it for himself.

Before entering the pawnshop on Rue Pierre-Charron where he'd accompanied Camille two or three times—she brought junk jewelry in to hock, and was always disappointed at the amount she got in return—he removed the watch from his wrist. At the window, they gave him four hundred francs. One year later, when his book was published, he showed up again at Rue Pierre-Charron to get back the watch and bring it to the Hotel Roma, where they'd surely know the name of the guest who had lost it, but he was too late. He had come several weeks after the deadline. Fifty years later, he still felt remorse over it, as that stolen, lost watch reminded him of the curious young man he'd once been.

*   *   *

He finished his book in the hotel room on Rue de la Voie-Verte and remained in the neighborhood. This empty, sleepy Paris in the month of August was in harmony with his state of mind, like the hidden beaches he'd discovered in July. He would have liked the summer never to end; he would continue to write in the heat and solitude.

Was it really solitude? Very early in the morning, and in the evening, he walked in those areas—La Tombe-Issoire, Montsouris, Rue Gazan, Avenue Reille—where you could feel the Parisian summer so strongly that you ended up melting into it and leaving behind any hint of solitude. You only had to let yourself flow haphazardly through the streets.

One evening, walking by Parc Montsouris, he entered a phone booth and dialed the number of the hotel on Quai de la Tournelle. He was calling from an island lost in the depths of summer.

"May I speak to Mlle Lucas?"

"To who? Could you repeat the name, please?"

He was amazed by the clarity of his interlocutor's voice, coming as it did from so far away. He repeated the name.

"We haven't heard from her in a month. She didn't even give notice she was leaving."

The man hung up. He had expected it. It was understandable. The moment he'd taken the train for the South on July 1, he'd felt certain that after that summer, nothing would ever be the same. And he'd been ever more certain on his return. The summer had erased all the preceding months, the way a photo exposed to sunlight gradually fades. The city he was coming back to gave the impression of both absence and expectation, or rather of suspended time. He was relieved of a burden that he'd thought he was condemned to carry on his shoulders for the rest of his life.

He called the apartment in Auteuil several times, but no one answered. Where had Kim and the child gone? And it was in the same phone booth, at the edge of Parc Montsouris and in the shade of the trees, that late one afternoon he dialed the number of the Hotel Chatham.

"May I please speak to Mr. de Gama?"

"What room number, sir?"

The man's voice was friendly, even mellow.

"He has no room number. He's one of the managers."

"Managers? I'm afraid I don't understand . . ."

The tone was sharper.

"I mean he's associated with the management of the hotel, with a Mr. Guy Vincent."

"Associated? Please hold the line, sir, I'm connecting you with the manager."

He waited a few minutes, during which he felt like hanging up. Entering the phone booth, he'd had a vague premonition that this was what they'd say, and that he'd dialed the number only to have it confirmed.

"How exactly can we help you, sir?"

The man had a deeper voice than the first one, with an accent from the Bordeaux region.

"I'd like to speak with Michel de Gama, a co-manager of that hotel with Guy Vincent."

"You must be joking, sir. I've never heard of those individuals. The only manager of this hotel is myself."

"Are you quite certain you don't know Michel de Gama? I find that rather surprising. I think you're hiding something."

"Hardly, sir. Good-bye, sir."

And the man hung up.

Bosmans left the phone booth and walked along Boulevard Jourdan. It was just what he'd expected and he couldn't suppress a laugh, which would have surprised him a few months earlier. He remembered the café at Saint-Lazare where he and Camille met up with Michel de Gama. And "Guy Vincent's office," which was indeed nothing but a scene from the Grévin Wax Museum. And his unease—his fear, really—the night Michel de Gama had chased after him at Porte d'Auteuil. And now, no one seemed to have heard of this man.

A late August afternoon, cooler than the day before, and with so little traffic that you could hear the rustling of the leaves. He walked by the Cité Universitaire. The students were probably away on holiday, and the buildings and lawns must have been deserted in the sunlight. He turned around and followed Rue Gazan.

The Pavillon du Lac was open and he sat at a table, on the terrace. He was the only customer. From an alley in Parc Montsouris, lower down, rose the sound of voices and children's shouts. The people he'd met that winter and spring now seemed so far away, shadows on a distant horizon . . . Except for the two afternoons when he'd rung at the door of the apartment in Auteuil and Kim had opened, the streets of Paris from those months would forever remain gray and black, because of his book, which had taken its inspiration from those people. He had stolen their lives, and even their names, and from now on they would exist only in the pages of that book. In real life, on the sidewalks of Paris, there was no longer any chance of running into them. Besides, summer had come, a summer unlike any he'd experienced before, a summer with light so limpid and intense that those phantoms had finally evaporated.

He dialed information to get the phone number of the house on Rue du Docteur-Kurzenne. Was it the same number as in the time of Rose-Marie Krawell and Guy Vincent? He dreamed for an instant that he would get one or the other "on the line," as they said back then. After all, you could dream of a line that time had spared, thanks to which you could get back in touch with those whom you'd lost track of.

Ring followed on ring with no answer. Was the phone still in the large bedroom on the second floor, where he had overheard Rose-Marie Krawell say: "Guy has just gotten out of prison"? When Guy Vincent occupied that room, Bosmans had noticed that the phone rang all the time and, whenever Guy Vincent answered, the conversation was brief. He didn't need to say a lot to get his message across. One Sunday afternoon, when the two of them were alone in the house, Guy Vincent had said to him, "If the telephone rings, you answer and tell them I'm in Paris." And he added, as if he suddenly regretted asking for such a favor: "You know, it's not really a lie, it's just a joke I like to play on my friends . . . " But in the end, Guy Vincent had not made him tell a lie, as the phone hadn't rung that day.

He again dialed the number of the house on Rue du Docteur-Kurzenne later that afternoon:

"Hello . . . who's calling, please?"

This time, someone had picked up immediately. A man's voice, deep. Bosmans was taken aback. He kept silent.

"Can you hear me?"

Then he said in a toneless voice:

"May I speak to Martine Hayward?"

And just the fact of saying that name plunged him back into the darkness and uncertainty of the previous months.

"You've got the wrong number. There's no one here by that name."

The answer made him feel relieved.

"I thought she had rented the house."

"No, definitely not, sir. It has never been for rent. It's been on the market for the past year."

"And yet, I visited the house with her several months ago. With a woman from the real estate agency."

He had spoken in a clear, firm voice. It surprised even him.

"The real estate agency? Which one, sir? Certainly not ours. I'm the only one handling this property."

He didn't know what to answer. A sentence came to mind: "The woman from the real estate agency was wearing a black blouse," the only clue he could provide, the only detail that would remain of that unknown woman until the end of time. But he was afraid the other would think he was pulling a prank and hang up on the spot.

"The rental agreement listed the name of the owner, Rose-Marie Krawell. I used to know Mme Krawell, a long time ago."

There was a pause. Then:

"You knew Mme Krawell?"

His interlocutor's voice had changed tone. It now expressed amazement.

"Yes. I even lived in that house. In the days when Mme Krawell also lived there. Fifteen years ago."

Another silence.

"What you're telling me is very interesting, sir . . . My agency has tasked me with selling this house . . . And it hasn't been easy . . . "

His interlocutor was on the verge of a confession. It might take only a few words to get him to talk.

"Not easy? I can imagine . . . Mme Krawell was a peculiar individual."

"I'll say. She left quite a tangled legacy when she died."

"Really?"

"We've been trying for months to straighten it out. But that woman was mixing in some very bad company.

Her file is thick. I don't mind telling you, sir, that it some-times feels hopeless."

"You said 'very bad company.' If you give me a few names, I might be able to provide some information."

"Can I trust you?"

The file must have been very thick indeed for him to blurt out that question, like a perfect stranger who asks you for help.

"A certain Mr. Heriford has complicated things . . . He and two friends of his."

"René-Marco Heriford?"

"That's the one. Do you know him?"

"A little bit. And I think I can guess the names of the two others: a certain de Gama and a fellow named Philippe Hayward."

The moment he spoke those names, Bosmans had doubts about their actual existence because of the novel he'd just finished writing, in which those three individuals were bit players.

"That's it . . . that's exactly right. Heriford, Hayward, and de Gama. I see you're aware of the situation. What's your name, sir?"

The question surprised him and roused his suspicion. So everything threatened to start over, just like the preceding months. They were setting a trap for him. He pictured Michel de Gama with his ear glued to the other extension, and the two others standing behind the real estate agent, who was seated in one of the armchairs in the large bedroom. And de Gama whispering what the man should say to draw him to the house.

"My name is Jean Bosmans."

He had said it like a dare. He felt like adding: "You can tell the three others standing near you that I have no intention of showing them the spot where Guy Vincent hid his treasure." But the sentence seemed so outdated, the past it evoked so distant, that he kept silent.

"Yes, sir, as I was saying, a very complicated situation . . . Heriford claimed to be Mme Krawell's godson and her only heir. It appears he embezzled a fair amount of money from his supposed godmother and even forged many of the documents . . . "

He was speaking faster and faster. No doubt he wanted to unburden himself of that "thick file" once and for all.

"The house was put in receivership, along with an apartment Mme Krawell owned in the Auteuil neighborhood. And we're awaiting final disposition . . . Heriford and his two friends have disappeared."

He thought as much, but still it was odd: disappeared just at the moment when he finished his book. And what about Kim and the boy?

"She really was mixing in bad company, that Mme Krawell, and you can imagine how difficult this has made it for us."

The man was growing increasingly talkative, as if he'd kept these things bottled up too long, but his voice was gradually becoming inaudible. Bosmans hung up. You can get bored with anything. And that morning, he had written the words "The End" on page 203 of his manuscript. He left the hotel and walked toward Boulevard Jourdan. He was no longer the same person. As he had drafted his book, page after page, a period of his life had melted away, or rather soaked into those pages as if into a blotter.

Disappeared: that was the word the man had used on the phone. Yes, disappeared: "Heriford and his two friends have disappeared."

He couldn't keep from repeating that sentence, and it made him feel like laughing. When he thought about it, most of the people he'd known in the past fifteen years had disappeared: Guy Vincent, Rose-Marie Krawell, so many others; and just one summer had also seen the sudden disappearance of Heriford, de Gama, Philippe and Martine Hayward, Camille Lucas aka Deathmask . . . All those phantoms from whom he'd taken inspiration to write his book.

These were fleeting, chance encounters. He hadn't had time to learn much about those people, who would forever remain enveloped in mystery—so much so that Bosmans wondered whether they weren't just figments of his imagination.

Over the following years, people had filled in previously unknown details about some of his characters, after coming across their names in his novels. It proved that the boundaries between real life and fiction were rather blurry. For instance, a detective from what they called the Vice Squad had written to say he was a reader of his books and that he'd in fact found mention in the police archives of René-Marco Heriford and his two friends, Michel de Gama and Philippe Hayward. Very little of interest, to tell the truth. Three young men who frequented the cafés around the Gare Saint-Lazare in the spring and summer of 1944 had been picked up on "various smuggling charges." Their names appeared in a few lines of the blotter at the Saint-Lazare station house. And a subsequent file, from General Information, indicated that in September 1944, "a certain Captain Heriford" had been spotted, "true identity unknown, wearing the uniform of an American officer despite his very young age," along with "his friends, Michel Degamat alias 'Renato Gama' and Philippe Hayward, in Resistance uniforms. All three individuals have priors. The alleged Heriford was lodging at 18 Rue Saint-Simon (Paris 6) in the home of a Mme Cholet, his mistress, who owned an 'antiques shop.'" Yes, very little of interest. And were such details, despite their apparent specificity, enough to prove that these three individuals had really existed?

Disappeared. And all that remained of them were half-erased traces in his book. He walked down Boulevard Jourdan, feeling even lighter than on his return to Paris six days earlier. He skirted Parc Montsouris, passed by the station for the Sceaux commuter rail, then Café Babel, where he noted that there were more customers than on previous days. It was probably the end of summer break for the residents of the Cité Universitaire. He couldn't remember ever having breathed so deeply. If he'd started to run, his breathing would have remained steady for hundreds and hundreds of meters, he who so often felt short of breath these last years.

Parked in front of the garage at Parc Montsouris was a convertible of English make. He felt like hopping inside and taking off without the ignition key, as a pal had shown him how to do when he was seventeen.

At Porte d'Orléans, he sat at the terrace of a café. He had finished his book, and for the first time he had the curious sensation of getting out of prison after years of incarceration. He imagined a man before whom the gates of La Santé opened wide, one sunny August morning. Bosmans crossed the street, entered the café opposite the jailhouse, sat at a table, and again he heard the little phrase that he'd overheard in his childhood and that had pursued him all his life: "Guy has just gotten out of prison."

After hesitating a few seconds, and still thinking about that man, he said to the waiter: "Two beers. With no head, please."

Thirty years later, on a spring afternoon, he went to the town hall in Boulogne-Billancourt to get a copy of his birth certificate, which he needed for a new passport. Leaving the town hall, he decided to walk up to Porte d'Auteuil.

There, crossing the boulevard, he noticed in front of him the glassed-in terrace of the restaurant Murat. And he recalled the night when, at the same place behind the window, seated at the same table, were Michel de Gama, René-Marco Heriford, and Philippe Hayward; then the image of Michel de Gama chasing him to the metro stop. He hadn't thought about them in years, or about when he'd known them; that period was so distant that it seemed as if someone else had lived it.

Suddenly, he found himself in a street he'd never gone back to. He stopped in front of the building, at whose door he had left Martine Hayward thirty years before. He had heard nothing further from her, nor from the others. Except for René-Marco Heriford, whom he'd seen, fifteen years earlier, in the Wimpy's on the Champs-

Elysées. He had sat next to him without saying anything. And he had noticed the watch on his wrist, the same "American army watch" whose mechanisms a stranger had shown him in his childhood—a stranger who was, he was now certain of it, Heriford himself.

He entered the building and knocked at the glass-paneled door of the concierge's lodge. The door cracked open, revealing the face of a man of about thirty.

"Can I help you, sir?"

"It was just for some information. Does Mr. Heriford still live on the fourth floor?"

"The apartment has been for rent for six months, sir."

How could that man have known Heriford's name? He wasn't even born at the time.

"For rent?"

He'd said it in such a brisk tone that the other looked startled.

"Are you interested? Would you like to see the apartment?"

"Very much."

The concierge pushed open one flap of the elevator's glass-paneled door to let Bosmans pass and pressed the button for the fourth floor.

The elevator rose as slowly as it had thirty years earlier.

"An old-style elevator," Bosmans said.

"Yes. Old-style," the concierge repeated without seeming to understand what the expression meant. Bosmans wondered what had become of Kim and the child after all these years. And he experienced such a sensation of emptiness that he thought the elevator had halted.

But when they arrived at the fourth-floor landing and the concierge took the key from his pocket and slid it into the lock, Bosmans put his hand on the man's shoulder.

"No . . . I'm sorry . . . Never mind . . . "

And before the other could even turn around, he was running down the stairs.

That night, he had a rather long dream. He was again running down the stairs of the apartment building in Auteuil after leaving the concierge on the landing, as he'd done the day before. Then he got into a car parked in front of the building, Martine Hayward's car. The key was on the dashboard. He took the same road as he had thirty years earlier with Camille and Martine Hayward, then with just Martine Hayward.

Soon he felt like he'd crossed a border and had arrived in the Vallée de Chevreuse, not because of the familiar landscape and the sudden freshness in the air, but rather it was as if he'd entered a zone where time became suspended, and moreover he verified this when he noticed that the hands of his watch had stopped.

The farther down the road he drove, the more he felt as if he'd returned to the heart of those endless summer afternoons of his childhood, when time wasn't suspended but simply immobile, and when you could spend hours watching an ant crawl jerkily around a wellhead.

After Chevreuse, he was tempted to take the wide forest path that led to the Moulin-de-Vert-Cœur Inn, but he decided against it. By now the inn must have been covered in forest vegetation. Especially Room 16.

A few miles more. The distance seemed shorter. He had already left behind the town hall of the village and the railroad crossing. After the public garden that ran alongside the railroad tracks, he noticed that the shutters on the small station were closed.

He parked the car on Rue du Docteur-Kurzenne. He was determined to enter the house. What could he possibly fear after thirty years? He rang. It was Kim who answered the door, as she had done thirty years earlier, when he rang at the door of the apartment in Auteuil. She hadn't changed. She smiled and said nothing, like people you once knew but whom you've never seen again. Except in your dreams. He asked where the boy was, but she didn't answer.

He bounded up the stairs. He wanted to avoid the second floor, the one with his old bedroom and the bedroom that Rose-Marie Krawell or Guy Vincent occupied when they were staying at the house.

He went directly to the third floor and entered the room with the skylight. A wall, still white and smooth, even at the precise spot where they had made a hole then plastered it up. He was now the only one who knew the location. And Guy Vincent's treasure would remain behind the wall, buried for all eternity. Gold ingots that were merely lead if you scratched the surface. Mailbags stuffed with wads of banknotes from the time of the black market, now obsolete. Ancient crates of smuggled American cigarettes.

He gazed through the skylight. Up there, the highest branches of a poplar were gently swaying, and the tree was signaling to him. An airplane glided silently in the blue sky, leaving behind it a trace of white, but it was impossible to tell whether it was lost, coming from the past, or else returning to it.

PATRICK MODIANO, winner of the 2014 Nobel Prize in Literature, was born in Boulogne-Billancourt, France, in 1945, and published his first novel, *La Place de l'Etoile,* in 1968. In 1978 he was awarded the Prix Goncourt for *Rue des Boutiques Obscures* (published in English as *Missing Person*), and in 1996 he received the Grand Prix National des Lettres for his body of work. Modiano's other writings in English translation include *Suspended Sentences, Pedigree: A Memoir, After the Circus, Invisible Ink, Paris Nocturne, Little Jewel, Sundays in August, Such Fine Boys, Sleep of Memory,* and *Family Record* (all published by Yale University Press), as well as the memoir *Dora Bruder*, the screenplay *Lacombe, Lucien,* and the novels *So You Don't Get Lost in the Neighborhood, Young Once, In the Café of Lost Youth,* and *The Black Notebook.*

MARK POLIZZOTTI has translated more than fifty books from the French, including works by Gustave Flaubert, Marguerite Duras, Arthur Rimbaud, Scholastique Mukasonga, and ten other volumes by Patrick Modiano. A Chevalier of the Ordre des Arts et des Lettres and the recipient of a 2016 American Academy of Arts and Letters Award for Literature, he is the author of eleven books, including *Revolution of the Mind: The Life of André Breton,* which was a finalist for the PEN/Martha Albrand Award for First Nonfiction; *Luis Buñuel's Los Olvidados; Bob Dylan: Highway 61 Revisited;* and *Sympathy for the Traitor: A Translation Manifesto*. His essays and reviews have appeared in the *New York Times,* the *New Republic,* the *Wall Street Journal, Apollo,* the *Nation, Parnassus, Bookforum,* and elsewhere. He directs the publications program at The Metropolitan Museum of Art in New York.